THE RECKONING

HOWARD OWEN

THE RECKONING

THE PERMANENT PRESS
Sag Harbor, NY 11963

For information, address:
    The Permanent Press
    4170 Noyac Road
    Sag Harbor, NY 11963
    www.thepermanentpress.com

Library of Congress Cataloging-in-Publication Data

Owen, Howard–
    The reckoning / Howard Owen.
        p.   cm.
    ISBN 978-1-57962-207-7 (hardcover : alk. paper)
        1. Fathers and sons—Fiction. 2. Male friendship—Fiction.
    3. Businessmen—Fiction. I. Title.

PS3565.W552R43 2010
813'.54—dc22   2010035768

Printed in the United States of America.

To Karen, as always

CHAPTER ONE

October 2003

They might have gotten rid of Butter, but he had been Carter's dog. And so he was allowed to stay, although neither he nor the two humans entrusted with his care seemed thrilled with the arrangement. Butter would go into the master bedroom every morning, looking inquisitively to the empty left side of the bed, then come back into the breakfast room, looking up at George or Jake. At first, they thought he would get over it, but then they both began to think that, if they lived in the house for another ten years and Butter lasted that long, he still would repeat this ritual every time he was let in the house.

After a while, they stopped letting him in, and he was relegated mostly to the doghouse and the fenced backyard, from which he occasionally escaped.

He would sit on the deck and watch them as they watched television, his mournful eyes finally forcing one or the other of them to close the blinds. They told themselves that at least he had the pleasure of the pool, where he would spend an hour at a time, dog-paddling, snapping at water bugs and barking at squirrels.

Neither father nor son ever said anything about getting rid of Butter, although he was, George admitted, a handful.

That morning, Butter had found a weak place in the fence and managed to loosen two of the vertical boards enough to squeeze through. Then, he had knocked over the trash can they kept outside the fence and had scattered its contents, including the remnants of the previous night's Chinese takeout, across the backyard.

George had left for work. All the while Jake was trying to clean up the mess, breathing through his mouth, Butter was licking him and trying to redistribute the mess he'd made.

Jake, already running late, remembered kicking sideways at the dog, causing Butter to give a surprised yelp. Within half a minute, though, he was back, tentatively pressing his nose against Jake's arm. Jake got most of the contents back into the plastic bag and then into the trash can. He led Butter back through the gap in the fence, but he could see that the dog looked back longingly at the outside world he'd just left.

Jake took him to the back screened porch and left him there for a minute. Inside, he retrieved the elastic leash they still had to use when they took Butter for walks. He led him back outside and tied one end of the leash to an oak tree near the doghouse, then attached the other to the dog's collar.

Jake remembers the look the dog gave him as he went inside to grab his books, hoping his ride hadn't left already. Butter always looked mournful when he realized he was being left behind, but there was something else that morning, it seemed to Jake later, a look of canine confusion.

"Stupid dog," Jake muttered.

That afternoon, Jake didn't get home until nearly 5. He'd caught a ride with two boys he didn't know that well, after cross-country practice. As he unlocked the front door, the sun threw shadows across the lawn. Jake turned down the thermostat in the stuffy house and heard the air conditioning kick in. He grabbed a bottle of Gatorade and drank half of it before he remembered Butter.

He wasn't in any particular hurry as he slid the glass door open, still holding the bottle in his hand. He wondered for a second, before he saw everything, whether he'd filled Butter's water bowl that morning. Not that he didn't drink all day from the chlorinated pool.

George had worried that the dog would drown some day "and I'll have to bury his ass in the backyard," but Carter had laughed and told him what he already knew: Labs were born to be in the water. They put a ramp at the shallow end where Butter could walk out when he got ready, and getting out of the pool was the one thing the dog seemed to learn quickly. He appeared able to stay afloat forever.

The first thing Jake saw that afternoon was the leash. One end was stretched taut from the tree, and the other disappeared over the lip at the deep end.

By the time he'd dropped the bottle and taken two tentative steps forward, he saw the flash of color as the sun hit the water. He walked rather than ran over, partly out of shock and partly because there didn't seem to be any point in hurrying.

Butter was floating, his eyes open. The chain probably had wrapped around his neck when he was thrashing about in the water. Maybe he went for a drink and fell in, or maybe it was just Butter being Butter, chasing a falling leaf's reflection, not realizing that he was connected to a leash that only allowed him five feet of leeway. It might have pulled at him, choking him, as he hit the water, and he might have tried to swim away from it, unable to get to the shallow end. Jake saw, before he ran, the scratches on the side of the pool and the blood there, and the dark floating material he didn't want to identify. He wondered how long Butter had been able to tread water, barking or whining.

Mom was wrong, Jake thought. You really can drown a Labrador retriever.

When he looked at Butter's lifeless, waterlogged body, after he had managed to pull it out of the pool, he could only think of his mother, at the hospital, and how much death looked the same. He hugged the cold body of the big dog, a dog he had never even felt a lot of affection for. It was, he knew, the last of Carter.

He walked back into the house, thinking about calling his father, or looking for a shovel, or maybe just waiting. And then, without really thinking about it, he started running. He didn't bother to lock the front door, wasn't even sure he had closed it.

He was wearing a sweatshirt and jeans along with his running shoes. He'd meant to shower when he got home. Now, running seemed like the right thing to do.

He left his West End neighborhood and then turned east toward downtown, with the sun getting lower, the late-afternoon light turning the hardwoods from brown and yellow into crimson and gold. He didn't even know where he was headed, just following his usual jogging trail by muscle memory.

9

By the time he got to the river, it was almost dark. Navigating his way down to the water and then up again to the pedestrian bridge, he still hadn't done much thinking. He had been trying very hard not to, pushing himself and focusing on breathing, losing himself in the rhythm of his lungs and legs, counting the distance. One step's a yard, a breath in and out equals six steps, six yards. Three hundred of those equal a mile.

Sometimes, when he was on training runs, he would run here, then walk across to the island before heading back. Today, all he felt was that the bridge led away, which was where he very much wanted to go. As long as he went forward, he didn't have to go back.

Then, walking along the bridge, the chill hit him. He looked west, to where the river curved. The sun, red and partially obscured by clouds, reflected off the water. He told himself not to stop, to start running again, keep going.

But he couldn't. The last few nature-lovers and doped-up-coming-down kids were making their way across the bridge, back to the mainland, and they might have noticed how odd he looked, standing there and staring into the day's last light. "Twilight's last gleaming," he muttered to himself.

He'd been pretty useless, at the end, he would try to rationalize, when he'd wake up at 5 A.M. and have to think about it. He was just a kid, after all. He was hurting, too. How could she do this to him?

The worst day, the one he could hold at arm's length after the sun came up, the one that was even worse than the day she left them, had been the day he didn't show up.

George had asked him to please go over to the hospital after school. George had a board meeting at 3:30 that he absolutely had to attend, and he wanted someone there with her all the time. For most of the last three weeks, after they moved her to the intensive care unit, it was George.

Jake hated it—the room full of strangers all wrapped up in their own private agonies, the cold professionalism of the doctors and nurses, but especially the sounds and sights and smells of the intensive care unit itself, the machines dutifully recording her demise. His mother drifted in and out of consciousness, and he convinced himself that she didn't really know or feel anything.

As school ended that day, a girl he had hung out with came up to him at his locker and said they were all going over to Trip Cooley's. Trip's parents were out of town for the week.

"Can't," Jake said, "gotta go be with my mom."

He felt so cheated. He knew there'd be major making out, maybe more, at Trip's. He saw the disappointment in the girl's eyes. He made a decision.

"Maybe I can go over for a few minutes. She won't miss me."

The girl's eyes brightened.

The Cooleys lived near the school, so they could walk to the impromptu party. Jake wouldn't stay long, and he could catch a city bus to the hospital afterward.

He took one toke, to be friendly, and he sipped a little beer. Jake was an athlete, but he wanted to be popular, too. He was sure no one could smell one beer. He and the girl wound up making out, and she let him feel her up a little, and then the beer bottle was empty and somehow he was holding another one.

The first fifteen minutes went by slowly, and he felt he could afford to stay fifteen minutes longer. He thought he had just glanced at his watch, which said 3:45, when he looked down and saw that it was almost 4:30.

"Gotta go," he said, failing in his first attempt to get up from the couch and his girlfriend. The other kids were amused at his sudden panic as he went out the front door, forgetting his books.

He had just missed one bus and had to wait almost twenty minutes for another. He walked and ran in the general direction of the hospital, three miles away, turning occasionally to see if the next bus was coming. He was reminded of the dream he always had, where he was late for some urgent appointment and couldn't get his legs to move properly.

By the time the bus caught up with him, he was only a mile and a half from the hospital, but he got on anyhow.

By the time he got to the ward, it was after 5. There had been some problem with Carter, the nurse said, and they had called his

11

father, who was on the way. Her look told Jake that she saw through to his very depraved soul, but said his mother seemed to be stable now.

Jake approached her. She seemed more bruised and bloated than usual, but at least she was resting, seemingly asleep.

But then she suddenly opened her eyes. And the look she gave Jake, part hurt and part forgiveness, was very much like the expression on Butter's lifeless, floating face. Like the nurse, he felt she knew what he'd been up to. She seemed to try to speak, but then she drifted off.

His father arrived ten minutes later. After being assured that Carter was past her latest crisis, he turned to Jake.

"Where were you?" he asked. Then, probably smelling the beer, he did something he hadn't done in a very long time. He hit Jake. It wasn't a slap or a punch or anything indicating forethought. He hit him in his sternum with the palm of his hand, pushing him back a foot and almost causing him to fall. Then George looked at him, near tears, before turning back to the bedside. They didn't speak for the rest of the day, and they never talked about that afternoon.

His mother never tried to speak to him again.

Now, finally coming to a full stop a third of the way across, Jake considered the river below. He saw an egret sitting on a rock, waiting. Between him and the sun, he saw the glint of a kayak being pulled from the river on the other side.

He didn't think of anything much, at least briefly successful in his goal. What he craved was action.

He stepped backward until he was leaning against the waist-high rail on the other side. When he went forward, he grabbed the bar in front of him and lifted himself up and over.

He clipped the top with his shoe as he crossed over and felt himself flipping, falling backwards into space, facing the dead blue sky. He even noticed the first star and had time to think "Venus" as he fell.

Chapter Two

September 2004

George James is walking through the Fan. He's forced himself to get up early and savor what he knows should be enjoyable. Now, he's wondering if he can catch a bus for the twenty-block ride back to the Warwick.

Still, he has to admit he's glad he made the effort, at least this once. The early morning light makes everything golden, although the leaves won't change for a month at least. These equinox days still give him a quiver of excitement. Fall has always been the season of What Could Happen.

It was still August when he left for college as a freshman. He was allowed to drive, with his father sitting beside him while his mother sat puffy-eyed in the backseat as they headed south.

It was a great disappointment to Wash James that his son and heir did not get into the University of Virginia, the alma mater to which he never gave another cent after George got his rejection letter.

The fallback school was New Hope, a liberal arts college in the Carolina Piedmont that was full of students who almost got into better institutions and whose parents were able to pay multiples of state-college tuition in exchange for what the school itself billed as a "Southern Ivy League education." "Whatever in the hell that is," Wash James muttered, but it was the best option for his son and heir.

George had been to the campus just once, on a forced march in which Wash took him to six schools in four days. George could hardly remember which one New Hope was.

13

"Boy," Wash said as he puffed on a Lucky Strike somewhere near the state line, "you're on your own now. I expect you to take everything you've been given and build on it. Make everyone understand that a James is something to be reckoned with."

George's father had a way of making him understand that anything he might ever achieve was the result of things beyond his influence—birth and money, mostly—while bad deeds were George's responsibility.

"It's down to you," the old man said. "It's your world to conquer."

It sounded much more like an imperative than an opportunity.

Washington James was at a critical point in his own life. He would run for the General Assembly next year, and win. He was positioning himself, even as he positioned his son, for greater things than just being the ham king.

THE REAPPEARANCE of Freeman Hawk, a ghost if ever there was one, has made George revisit the days when he thought he was surely growing into the kind of man he wanted to become, more noble if less rich than his father and a damn sight happier.

George wouldn't have recognized him if he hadn't given his name over the intercom. Even then, he had to pause for a second before accepting that Freeman Hawk was standing in the lobby of the Warwick, in the flesh.

He was hairless and tattooed, with the tail of some creature running down his arm from his sleeveless shirt. He looked as if he hadn't gained an ounce in thirty-three years. He might even have lost a pound or two.

The name he was going by, he said, was Chris Rainier, and it took George a few seconds to dredge that one up from his memory bank.

Freeman Hawk told him that what he needed was a place to hide.

George told Jake most of the story, four nights ago—who Chris Rainier really was and why they were more or less "harboring" him. He repeated the story Jake has heard so many times, about him and Freeman Hawk. Freeman mostly just sat and listened. Jake has heard about George's old friend for most of his life, living pure and unfettered somewhere in the pristine north. It was hard to believe that the emaciated, tattooed, slightly nervous man sitting across from him was the great Freeman Hawk.

"Sometimes I wish I'd gone with him," George would say when he told the story of how he "almost got away"; then laugh and squeeze Carter and say, "but then where would you be?"

"Single and happy," his mother would say, and they would laugh, but it always troubled Jake somehow that his father almost left them all, before he was even born, for Canada.

The trouble, George said, explaining Freeman Hawk's appearance on their doorstep with an assumed name, sprang from Freeman's opposition to yet another U.S. adventure, which Freeman referred to as "Bush's goddamn war"; and the American authorities having power to reach even into a foreign country to "get" him.

"So, like, why did you come down here? Back to the U.S.?" Jake asked.

"Good question," Freeman Hawk said, nodding as if he himself was stumped by this maneuver. Until now, he had let George do most of the talking.

"I figured," he said, "that this would be the last place they'd be looking for me, especially with the aid of my trusty alter ego."

"Chris Rainier," George said, shaking his head and laughing. Freeman smiled, too.

"What?" Jake asked.

His father explained that Chris Rainier had been one of the first black basketball players at New Hope, a school whose fraternities felt comfortable as late as the spring of 1968 holding an Old South parade down the town of New Hope's main street, replete with frat boys in Confederate uniforms, hoop-skirted sorority belles and rebel flags.

Chris Rainier made all-conference at guard his sophomore year. Shortly afterward, he was arrested for leading a band of students and townies, almost all black, into the middle of the last of the antebellum parades. The ensuing melee sent several on each side to the hospital and left a Scarlett O'Hara imitator cowering behind a severely mistreated Plymouth GTX, her green gown ripped and ruined.

"They'd have let him back in if he'd only apologized," George said, enjoying the memory, "but he wouldn't back down an inch.

"He graduated from Winston-Salem State and finally got his law degree. He's still raising hell down there, from what I read, fighting the good fight."

"And," Freeman said, warming to the story, "he gave up what he called his 'white-ass so-called Christian name' when he went Black Muslim.

"So, since he wasn't using his name anymore, I figured I might as well borrow it."

Jake promised not to tell anyone. He looked at his father, though, and then at Freeman Hawk, and he couldn't shake the feeling that George was in over his head.

As George gives up on catching a bus and starts walking again, something—the smell of decaying leaves, the sun painting the maples, a distant church bell—reminds him of the day he met Freeman Hawk.

His parents accompanied him up to his second-floor dorm room that first day. There were twenty double rooms on each floor, all half the size of the one George had to himself in his parents' Georgian brick home off Cary Street.

Only two other boys from St. Christopher's were going to New Hope, and George was not that close to either of them, so he had decided to accept whichever roommate was assigned.

For George, this departure from privacy and habit was not easy.

He had learned all the social and academic lessons young future leaders of Richmond were expected to absorb, and he had a certain amount of savoir-faire. He had been to Europe twice. He owned a tuxedo. He knew the bread went on the left and the water went on the right. He was able to converse easily with adults and the young women in his social circle.

But beneath the polish, George James was and always would be shy. That was why he decided to take potluck, try something different, push himself.

His parents would've preferred that he room with someone he knew, or at least someone whose parents they knew. Clara tried to get him to room with Freddie August from Tappahannock, because she and Freddie's mother had gone to St. Margaret's together.

In the end, though, George got his way, something that rarely happened.

"What kind of a name is that? Hawk? What the hell is that?" Wash wanted to know later, when the three of them were alone.

"Well," Clara said hopefully, "his first name is Freeman. Maybe he's related to Douglas Southall Freeman." Her voice drifted off as she realized how unlikely it was that Freeman Hawk was related to a Richmond newspaper editor and historian.

George's roommate was already there when they hauled the first load of his possessions up the steps and down the hall, second door on the left. Freeman Hawk, the first time George and his parents saw him, was hanging from the door frame doing pull-ups. He was wearing the first tie-dyed

17

T-shirt George had ever seen, along with a pair of boxer shorts. He had a Mohawk haircut.

"Oh," he said, when he realized he had an audience, "sorry." He let himself down, and they followed him into the small room that would be home to Wash and Clara's son until they could arrange to get him moved. A Fuggs poster hung on the wall; the Grateful Dead played in the background on a small portable stereo.

He was seventeen, tall and skinny and quiet. He told them his name. They asked him where he was from and he said "Alto," as if anyone would know where Alto, North Carolina, was. Pressed, he said it was just a few miles away, toward Siler City. Wash James just nodded his head. It was strange to his parents, and to George himself a little, that the boy from a North Carolina town nobody had ever heard of spoke with almost no accent at all.

Freeman Hawk's parents weren't there and hadn't been there. An uncle had brought him and his very few belongings—the clock radio and the stereo and two bags of clothes, mostly—in a pickup truck.

"Oh," he replied to Clara's question, "we said goodbye back home. And they just live half an hour away." Then he excused himself and disappeared down the hall.

George, his thrill over impending freedom dampened a little by the realization that he really was leaving home, walked his parents back to the car and twice rejected their offer to take him to dinner somewhere, anywhere in town. He watched the Lincoln disappear into the green distance.

George wasn't sure at all that he shouldn't have opted for a roommate he knew, even Freddie August if it came to that. His classmates in prep school had been mostly of a type, and Freeman Hawk definitely was not that type.

Back in the room, Freeman had returned and was already reading Look Homeward, Angel because he knew he would be expected to for his freshman English class. George wandered down the corridor and met some of his new classmates.

When he came back, the room was empty. He accepted an invitation from the boys across the hall to go get a burger.

Freeman Hawk came back in sometime after 2, waking George, who was definitely not used to having a stranger enter his room in the middle of the night, especially one wearing a Mohawk.

"Jesus!" he said, already bolt upright beside his bed as Freeman stepped back, seemingly as surprised as George. "You scared the shit out of me!"

He couldn't help noticing, though, that Freeman Hawk did not appear to be drunk, didn't even seem to have alcohol on his breath.

They eventually became attuned to each other's rhythms. George even had dinner with him a few times. As they eased into the fall semester, he became less and less inclined to do what he thought of doing that first night—changing roommates.

New Hope had started as a Quaker school, and it had better intentions than most southern colleges when it came to race relations.

Still, in the fall of 1967, there were only about fifty black students in a student body of almost 5,000.

One of them was Andre McQueen.

He seemed to be, as one boy put it, "neither one thing nor the other." His skin was an orangish-pink, topped with an impregnable tangle of orange hair. He seemed to be an oddity and a pariah to both the black and white students, an African-American student who wasn't a star athlete. And he lived in Satterwhite Hall, one floor above George and Freeman.

"Must have been a white man in the woodpile," a dorm mate said once, almost out of Andre McQueen's earshot as he walked past. George laughed a little, enough to get along.

It was a surprise when he came back from a psychology class one Wednesday afternoon and found Andre McQueen in his room, actually stretched across his bed, talking with Freeman.

The black student sat up, then stood quickly as if he'd been caught in some despicable act. Freeman introduced him to George, who mumbled a hello and then went out again, returning an hour later to find Freeman alone.

George didn't speak for five minutes. Finally, Freeman asked him if anything was wrong.

George blurted it out.

"What the hell are you doing asking that—that . . ."

"Nigger?" Freeman asked quietly.

"I wasn't going to say that, and you know it." He blushed.

"You know," Freeman Hawk said, "if you go to college and all you do is spend four years farting around with PLUs, you've wasted your father's money. You want to stretch yourself a little."

PLUs, George knew already, were People Like Us.

Freeman had said it quietly, no accusation in his voice. Still, it chafed George to be made to feel like such an asshole.

"That guy," he said, "he just bugs me. He's not normal. He never speaks to anybody. He's stuck up."

Freeman laughed for a full minute, until it looked as if George might have to fight him over it.

"Stuck up? Damn, George. He's been shunned. Guys leave the bathroom when he comes in. And I'll tell you something else. He's probably the smartest guy in this dorm. He's on a full scholarship, you know that? He can speak four damn languages, and he wants to major in physics. Expand your world a little bit, man."

Freeman, George knew, was on a scholarship, too, one of a dozen Williams Scholars at New Hope, everything paid for. The well-to-do majority at the school only grudgingly accepted the bright but needy ones on grants. George respected his roommate's intelligence, but he still assumed the two of them would have less and less in common once freshman rush separated them. Freeman had been so contemptuous of fraternity life when George had asked him where he planned to pledge that the question had not been raised again.

"I wasn't shunning him," George said, aware of how whiny he sounded.

They argued about race and religion and politics. George, with his top-dollar private-school education, soon came to realize that he was no match for the pride of Alto, North Carolina, where everybody in the county went to the one public high school except the handful of true believers whose parents had started a private, unaccredited, all-white Christian school.

George was no firebrand. He was, his father told people at the club, "easily led." Wash James' biggest worry was that the forces of communism and integration that found such a friendly haven on college campuses would take over his leadership role.

George had no quick answers for most of his roommate's arguments. In fact, he was somewhat appalled to learn, in his first modern civilization class, that the United States apparently had stolen Panama and, before that, Cuba. He thought at first that his professors and Freeman Hawk were conspiring to brainwash him, but at some point, the sheer weight of all those people with more intelligence and/or education brought him to the conclusion that he and his family (and many of his PLU friends at New Hope) had been wrong about some if not many things.

Visits home at Thanksgiving and Christmas were tense. George argued with Wash about almost everything until finally Clara asked him privately not to talk about "things like that" in front of his father.

"Do you want him to have a stroke?" she asked.

Wash James blamed most of it on the new roommate, and he was eager for his son to pledge when the new semester started. A room at a good fraternity house would straighten him out, Wash was sure.

George worked hard that first semester and pulled a 3.2 grade point average, certainly acceptable to him and his parents. Freeman Hawk, who did all his studying somewhere other than in their room, adamantly refused to divulge his GPA, and George wondered if his roommate hadn't fucked off the first semester, using all his intellectual muscle to convert him. Finally, he enlisted the aid of a friend who worked in the admissions office.

"Jesus, man," the friend said. "My advice? Take whatever he's taking, and sit beside him during tests."

Freeman Hawk had pulled a 4.0.

George had become comfortable around Andre McQueen, the first black person with whom he had ever had anything resembling an equal relationship. George learned that the joking, jiving faux friendliness he affected with the domestic help or the black people working at his father's company didn't go very far with Andre. Unlike other African-Americans of George's limited acquaintance, Andre McQueen wanted to be taken seriously, insisted on it, really.

Freeman's other friends were an odd lot, surely not rush material. There was a boy from New Jersey who wore a Beatles haircut and black Buddy Holly eyeglasses and majored in inappropriate conversation. Another one, a country kid from western North Carolina, was openly gay, which made George wonder, guiltily, about Freeman Hawk's sexual orientation.

And there were the Scag Sisters. That's what some of the other Satterwhite residents called the two bleach-blond sophomores who always seemed to be around Freeman whenever George saw him on campus. They were not sisters, and they were not at all unattractive. They were just— like Freeman and most of the crowd that seemed to gravitate to him—different.

There was no co-ed visitation yet at Satterwhite, but one night George came back from a drunken blind date to find both the girls, along with Freeman and the gay boy, Tim Fairweather, in the dorm room, sharing a gallon bottle of Bali Hai.

George wondered if they were going to stay the night, if he would be the nervous but willing party in some kind of orgy like the ones he'd heard about, the ones he imagined when he would turn quietly on his side in the darkened room and reach for the only sexual companion he'd known yet.

Sober, George would have felt like a fifth wheel, but he was discovering what a convenient social tool alcohol was. However, when he put his arm around the more comely of the twins, who was after all sitting on *his* bed, she stopped him gently but discouragingly.

Soon, the other three left. Freeman sneaked them down the same stairs they'd ascended. He never seemed to get caught.

Back in the room, he acted surprised that George thought it was "amazing, fucking amazing" that he had sneaked two girls into their room.

"As long as nobody does anything they don't want to do, what's the harm?" he said, shrugging.

People in the dorm wondered loudly about Freeman Hawk's sexual persuasion. The Scag Sisters, the logic went, were lesbians anyhow, and Tim Fairweather was a fag, and who the hell knew what Andre McQueen was?

George would eventually find out where Freeman Hawk went when he would disappear for a day or two at a time. On George's nineteenth birthday, Freeman told him he was taking him out for a birthday treat. That's how he described it: "birthday treat," as if George were a five-year-old. But, intrigued, he went along.

They walked across campus to a shady street a block off the main drag. One of the Scag Sisters answered the door and led him in.

He looked back at Freeman Hawk, somewhat panicked. "I'll come get him after a while," he said. "Be gentle with him."

No one in George's crowd would admit to being a virgin, but everyone pretty much knew who was and who wasn't. George himself didn't know sometimes how it was going to work itself out. The girl from Greensboro he dated that fall would let him touch her with his fingers, more out of duty than lust, and give him some relief with hers, but there was a wall there that George was sometimes afraid he would never break down.

So he owed Freeman Hawk a large debt of gratitude he could never truly acknowledge. He could only smile as knowingly as possible and say the sisters were great. He did not, however, ever refer to either of them as the Scag Sisters again.

He wanted to ask Freeman Hawk how he had managed to so completely win the affection of two sophomore girls, but that would have betrayed a lack of sophistication that his pride wouldn't allow. He was a senior before they could look back and laugh about it all.

George did pledge that January. He settled on Sigma Nu, a party frat that had the right boys in it. Wash had been a Sigma Nu at Virginia. At first, he seemed to "fit right in," just as Wash said he would.

Some things did bother him, though. An upperclassman would tell a racist joke, sometimes within careless earshot of one of the middle-aged black maids who kept the three-story brick Georgian house from collapsing under the weight of its own beer cans and vomit. And George would think about Andre McQueen, or the black guy in his chemistry class who wore a coat and tie to class every day while everyone else began slouching, shirttails out, into the late sixties.

He neither approved nor complained, rationalizing that as a pledge he had no standing. He was still living in the dorm. He wouldn't move to "the Zoo" until the next fall, and he found the cultural bends brought on by splitting his time between fraternity life and Freeman Hawk almost unbearable.

That spring, the first of the women (and they were all women) began appearing in front of the New Hope post office. They were older, faculty wives mostly, and they were against a war George James was aware of only as a nuisance, something he was sure would be over long before he had to deal with it. Freeman Hawk was against the war, of course. George, whose father regaled him with tales of World War II and duty, did not think Vietnam was wrong. It was just inconvenient.

The protestors did not speak. They stood at a spot where most of New Hope's students passed between campus and town, eliciting giggles and ignoring occasional crude comments along the lines of "Go back to Russia" or "traitor." For the most part, the students were afraid to say too much. No one knew exactly which professors' wives were standing there.

They were only there on Wednesdays, noon until 2. Not one student joined them the first four weeks. Dissent was not part of New Hope's makeup, even though the school had been founded by Quakers. Dissent was rude.

The fifth week, George was walking along with two fellow Sigma Nu pledges, headed for the Rathskellar in lieu of his afternoon psych class, when one of his new friends said, "Holy shit. They've got some damn recruits."

George looked up ahead. The small group at the post office had doubled in size, and most of the "recruits" were Freeman Hawk and his compatriots. Tim Fairweather, the Scag Sisters, Andre McQueen and another black guy, plus two others George didn't know.

Freeman's sign: "Their war/your blood."

The passing students were harassing their peers with insults that manners and fear would not allow them to inflict on the older women. "Whores!" shouted a boy in a passing car. "I'll do you for free," Tim Fairweather shouted.

The other fledgling Sigma Nus joined the mildly hostile crowd. George hung back, hoping neither the pledges nor Freeman Hawk would notice him.

Freeman did. He didn't look upset or disappointed, though. He just flashed a "V" that still meant "victory" in George James' world.

They argued about the war, and war in general, that spring, especially after Freeman joined the protests. It was one topic on which George would not budge. His father had risked his life in World War II, and he was damned if he was going to turn into some kind of cowardly peacenik. Besides, he couldn't give in to Freeman Hawk on everything, could he?

When George went home to Richmond at the end of spring semester, resigned to another summer of working for his father, he and Freeman Hawk said their goodbyes as friends, but there were no plans to visit. Come fall, Freeman would be in an apartment and George would be in Sigma Nu.

A little youthful rebellion, Wash James told his golfing friends, was OK, as long as it didn't get out of hand.

CHAPTER THREE

He almost falls as he runs up the front steps. He's been late too often in his brief time at Barton. In some ways, it's easier to cut a whole class than to show up a minute late. He's relieved that Mr. Epps doesn't seem to care that he slips into his seat at least ten seconds after the bell stops ringing.

The bar is not quite as high at Barton as it was at the magnet school. There, everyone was expected to be accepted at U.Va. or William and Mary or, at minimum, to earn a significant scholarship to some lesser school. At Barton, some of the kids won't even be going to college, and many will attend private universities where tuition rather than academic standards is the biggest barrier.

"If worse comes to worse," George assured him one time over the summer, "there's always New Hope. It ain't U.Va., but it ain't bad." (George remembered, as he said it, his father saying almost the same thing to him.)

Jake knows his father is spending more money for less education since the expulsion. There are five others here at Barton who were expelled from his old school. They don't socialize, as if they are too embarrassed by their mark of shame, the scarlet "F" for "fuckup," as Jake thinks of it.

Jake can't work up much enthusiasm for any of his classes. He has been persuaded to run cross-country, his reputation having preceded him from the magnet school. Running, he believes, helps him keep whatever sanity he might have. He still has fits of anger, still thinks too much about the past, still sleeps too much. He's overheard Carrie tell his father that perhaps he should be on some kind of antidepressant. His father's response, through the thick Warwick walls, was indecipherable but sounded disturbingly noncommittal.

Jake looks around the room, once he's caught his breath. Andrea is seated in the next row over, toward the back. She wiggles her fingers on her desktop and winks when he looks back. He smiles, relieved that she hasn't realized overnight what a loser he is.

Despite the hovering possibility of a beat-down by her former boyfriend, Jake is glad to have rediscovered Andrea Cross. She is the prime antidepressant in his life right now. They don't date, just hang out together in and out of school, and they haven't gone as far sexually as Jake would like. However, it is obvious to their classmates that they prefer each other's company, and that Pete Fallon is in the embarrassing position of having to endure his girlfriend being stolen by the new boy.

It seems to Jake that everyone at Barton has taken sides on the Jake-Andrea-Pete issue, and he's constantly surprised at some act of unexpected hostility or support by some student he doesn't even know.

The class, consisting mostly of give-and-take between teacher and pupils on "the true meaning of freedom as envisioned by the founding fathers," goes by quickly enough.

"Maybe if you set that alarm just five minutes earlier, you'd be able to get to class on time and comb your hair," Andrea says as she comes up from behind. "Maybe even wash your face. You're a mess." She reaches up and flicks some sleep matter out of the corner of his eye.

He blushes. He's glad that they're comfortable enough, some residue of the childhood intimacy they once shared in the old neighborhood, so that she can talk to him like this. Sometimes he thinks he must send vibrations to others, creating an invisible barrier. He has had a lot of space in the last twenty months.

"Thanks," he says to her, and she looks surprised.

"For what?"

He shrugs, giving her a quick kiss on the forehead, and walks her to her second-period class, then goes down the hallway to his.

From January of 2003 until his expulsion fifteen months later wasn't a free fall. There was the occasional updraft, but it was the exception.

He'd been a straight-A student through the first half of the ninth grade, but then his mother got very sick very quickly, and everything fell apart. He had been a state age-group swim champion before he took up cross-country. The harder the work involved, the more likely Jake was to succeed, Carter Bessette James told George once, when their son was only twelve and had a meltdown because a dental appointment caused him to miss swim practice for the first time in more than a month.

"He needs to make a mistake once in a while, just so he knows it won't kill him," she said.

After the funeral, Jake went back to school and was treated with arm's-length consideration, allowed to miss homework assignments or practice. People, he realized, were unwilling to confront him. After a short lifetime of striving to always be the best, he found it strangely comforting to wallow in something entirely different, to intentionally obliterate expectations.

Jake was, George told friends, mad at the world.

He quit the track team, and his grades suffered, but he got through ninth grade. There were incidents the fall of his sophomore year. He'd meant to do better, and he was on the cross-country squad again, winning three meets in a row, until what his father called (when he called it anything) "that thing on the bridge."

He missed a rock the size of a Buick by no more than five feet, he was told later, and it was his good fortune that a couple of college students from VCU were on the ground beneath the pedestrian bridge and were able to reach him. He never lost consciousness, but the impact with the water, as his body twisted so he hit it chest-first, knocked the breath out of him.

He was kept overnight at the hospital with a broken nose and a few other cuts and bruises. George didn't ask him anything of substance, didn't even ask him what happened to Butter, until they came home the next afternoon.

"Why?" he asked when they were inside, before Jake could even take off his bloodstained jacket. He couldn't hold the question in any longer. "What were you thinking?"

Nobody used the word "suicide." They just thought it. Jake had told the policeman who questioned him that he was sitting on the railing and slipped. He could see that neither the cop nor his father believed him.

"It just seemed like the thing to do," Jake shrugged and turned to go to his room. His father spun him around and slapped his face, just missing the nose that still throbbed and would need surgery when the swelling went down.

Father and son both stood staring at each other for a couple of seconds, one as stunned as the other. When Jake turned around again, George grabbed him around his waist and hung on as if he might otherwise drown.

"Goddammit, don't you do this to me!" he said. "I can't take anymore goddamn losses right now. You think you're at the end of your rope? Take a number, pal."

Jake crumpled onto the floor, and he and his father sat there, huddled with their foreheads touching, for a long time. Jake had never seen his father cry before. Even at the funeral, he had sat frozen, squeezing his son's hand, staring straight ahead, never blinking. Afterward, he received old friends with all the grace his breeding demanded. Jake had hated him for that.

Jake could not tell you, even now, that he absolutely, positively meant to end his young life in the James River that beautiful fall afternoon. Butter's drowning certainly triggered something, and he had been feeling hard-pressed to "just keep putting one foot in front of the other," the way George advised. He was weary of the long march and felt he was merely wearing a dog's path around the phantom of his former life.

Jake had never told his father or anyone else how much he missed his mother. It would have been awkward. It wasn't cool. When a girl or some guy he didn't know expressed regrets about his loss, he'd shrug and say, "Those things happen" or "Everybody's got to go sometime" or, worse, "She was so bad off, it was a blessing." He knew that, to him, even the loss of the Carter Bessette James who lay there at the end, being eaten alive by her own traitorous body, was no blessing that he could appreciate.

The first thing he remembers after his jump was one of the VCU students giving him mouth-to-mouth and pressing down on his chest. It's funny, but Jake sees the student once in a while. It's inevitable, living right off campus. It makes him feel awkward, embarrassed. The one time he came around a corner and came face-to-face with the guy, he had the impression the feeling was very much mutual.

Nobody officially called it an attempted suicide, but he had the feeling, at the magnet school, that everyone knew. Jake is grateful that his new classmates at Barton only know the sketchiest details, probably provided by his fellow outcasts. He's only shared the story with Andrea.

After he recovered, Jake did go to a few sessions with the shrink, who never mentioned his jump. He supposes their "visits" must have helped some, although he never experienced any kind of breakthrough that he could identify.

Last Christmas was a disaster, all agreed. They were selling the house. George couldn't bear to live there anymore. Without the barely tolerated Butter, father and son discovered at last its eternal emptiness.

Perversely, though, Jake insisted that they stay.

31

"You're wallowing," George told him.

So Jake ran away the day after Christmas, intending to move in with Tyler down in Oaxaca. He actually got there, on George's American Express card, and there were many tense phone conversations and eventually promises of clemency, before his aunt sent him back.

When George picked him up at the airport in Richmond two days after New Year's, he informed him that they had already moved, to the Warwick. To this day, Jake has not gone back to look at the house where he spent most of his first fourteen years. He's beyond being angry anymore and has even admitted to his father that it was time to go. Plus, he has come to secretly enjoy his status as the only teenager in a 1920s high-rise full of doting surrogate aunts. But, in truth, he's afraid he might do something embarrassing, like cry, if he went back there with his father, sitting in the car and watching somebody else's family sit by the pool or laugh and talk around the breakfast table on the screened side porch.

The rest of the winter and early spring of his sophomore year, Jake's grades improved somewhat, and he was on the track team. He still was what his father referred to as out of control, but there was reason for optimism.

Jake, though, didn't feel comfortable anymore with his friends at the magnet school, and he tried to avoid anyone from the old neighborhood. There was too much history, too many strange looks, too many concerned voices asking, "How're you doing, Jake?" He drifted toward other kids, the ones who somehow communicated to each other that they had been wronged beyond all compensation, and had a right to stand to one side and despise the world that had shorted them in some fashion. He had earned his membership with his leap from the bridge.

The car was nothing special, a 1993 Honda Accord, burgundy, automatic transmission.

Jake had learned to drive reasonably well, with his new best friend, Leon Custalow, as his instructor. Leon would let him practice on Leon's foster parents' car, when they were both at work. Leon was sixteen and knew where the extra set of keys was hidden. They'd go out to the parking lot at Target and drive back and forth, Leon urging him to take chances. George kept talking about how Jake, who had missed driver's ed the year before, needed to sign up for lessons. Jake figured he'd wait until his sixteenth birthday to let him know he could drive already, when he would announce that he was ready to go get his license.

Spring in Virginia is much overrated, doled out in dribs and drabs. On Wednesday, warm zephyrs may whisper clouds away from a cerulean sky, but on Thursday and Friday, the rains come. The weekend brings a cold snap that kills the spirits of overly optimistic gardeners and ruins many a long-planned wedding.

So, when just such a perfect Wednesday availed itself to all of Richmond in early April, Leon Custalow was able to persuade Jake to seize the day.

They walked in the front door of their school and they walked out the back, simple as that.

"I know a couple of girls over at Tucker. I bet they'd come with us," Leon said. Tucker was the public school Leon attended before being chosen for the magnet school for his sophomore year. He was a big guy who claimed to be part Indian. He was bright but was struggling in class, over his head for the first time in his life.

Jake shrugged. By this time, he had dyed his hair black and was wearing a trench coat to school every day, same as Leon, but he had not "been around." From the stories Leon told, Jake knew he was no virgin, and he was vaguely afraid of the kind of sullen, knowing, wise-beyond-their-years girls Leon might talk into skipping with them. Jake, ever hopeful, had been carrying a rubber in his wallet for almost a year. He wondered if it still worked.

"Whatever," he said. "Sounds good to me."

Leon wasn't able to get one of the girls on his cell phone until the break after first period.

"Come on," he said. "The sun's shining, the sap's rising. . . . Aw, you've got a dirty mind."

They talked awhile longer, then Leon nodded enthusiastically.

"OK." Pause. "OK. The parking lot at noon. Be there, sweet pants."

He gave Jake the thumbs-up.

They borrowed the Honda, the same one in which Leon had taught Jake to drive. They borrowed a couple of six-packs, too. They sat in the Tucker parking lot until almost 1, drinking one beer each, saving the rest for the party. Every time Leon called the girl he'd talked to earlier, her phone was off.

"Shit," Leon said, sighing and shrugging. "I guess they couldn't get away. Prick tease."

So much of the day had been wasted already. When Jake considered the consequences—and there surely would be consequences—he could almost feel the rain and chill that would descend when George found out.

"Screw it," Leon Custalow said. He took the key out of the ignition and tossed them in Jake's lap. "Here. You drive. Let's go somewhere and get fucked up."

Jake had only driven twice on public streets so far, but he didn't want to be a wuss. They started on a second beer each when it became obvious that the girls weren't coming. Jake tried to hide a grimace as he swallowed. He had developed neither a tolerance nor a taste for alcohol. Already once in March, George had been summoned to bring him home sick and unruly from an unchaperoned party in the West End.

He and Leon switched sides, and Jake started the Honda.

"Where to?"

"The river! To the river!"

34

A couple of times, Jake had been to the places where you could wade to flat, wide rocks in the James that were big enough to allow several people to sit and drink. In summer, you could jump or wade off into the water to cool off. But it was early April.

"Think anybody'll be there today?" he asked.

"Oh, yeah. Lots of screw-ups like us. Everybody'll be skipping on a day like this."

Everybody, Jake thought, except those hot girls from Tucker.

He was only slightly discomfited by the knowledge that "his" bridge probably would be within eyesight of where they were going.

They were headed down Belvidere, with Jake watching the speedometer anxiously and Leon working on his third Miller, when the police car just seemed to materialize behind them. Leon could see from the look in Jake's eyes what the problem was. He didn't even have to look back.

"Just be cool," he said, leaning down slightly to slide the half-full beer under the seat. "You're not doing anything wrong. Just be cool."

"Turn here," he said as they neared the exit that would lead them down to the parking lot by the river. He said it when they were only fifty feet away, and Jake had to slam on the brakes and try to make a ninety-degree turn at thirty-five miles an hour. If the city had gotten around to putting power lines underground, it might have worked out all right. Jake clipped the pole as he cut too sharply, damaging the right front headlight as the siren behind them gave a short burst. The pole itself fell directly on the Honda, and everyone said later it was a miracle neither of the boys was seriously injured. It crushed the roof between where they were sitting.

"Run!" Leon said, and Jake, not knowing what else to do, obeyed. They got all the way to Hollywood Cemetery before three other cars full of cops looking for some excitement on a slow spring day surrounded them. One of them tackled

Leon as he ran between ancient tombstones, while Jake hid behind another one. Leon seemed to think it was funny when they finally handcuffed him and hauled him away.

"Come on out, son," a tired-looking, gray-haired police officer said, looking right at the stone behind which Jake was cowering. He finally did, reluctant as much because he had wet himself as from fear of punishment.

It turned out that Leon was not with his foster family anymore. He'd been kicked out just two days before and was living in a shelter. He'd had a house key made before that happened, and before they began to suspect him of stealing from them.

The bill of particulars against Jake was impressive: car theft, driving without a license, reckless driving, driving while intoxicated (even though he only made it to .04 on the Breathalyzer test), underage drinking, resisting arrest, possession of marijuana (Leon's) and possession of stolen goods. This last one had to do with the antique clock Leon had taken when they "borrowed" the car.

Leon was not inclined to suffer alone. He said they were in it together, that Jake knew he'd been kicked out of the house and the car was stolen.

George threatened to let Jake stay in jail until the trial, but after one night he employed the services of Anderson Stokes, a fellow member of the Commonwealth Club and his lawyer.

Leon's past was not without blemish. (The magnet school principal said the school would do better character checks in the future.) It was easy for Stokes to portray Jake as an impressionable young boy, still reeling from the death of his beloved mother.

When it was all over, Jake got two years suspended and a couple of hundred hours of community service, while Leon went to a youth offenders camp. Jake has not heard from him since the day they left court, Leon headed for a delousing and Jake going back to the Warwick. "Pussy," Leon sneered at him as they parted.

There was malicious amusement around town over two magnet school boys doing such a despicable thing. It was no surprise to either Jake or his father when George received a certified letter from the school notifying him that Jake was expelled.

It seemed like the last step down a trail he'd been descending since his mother died. He felt real shame over what had happened. He saw the disappointment in the eyes of the Aunts and the other older people at the Warwick. He could hear their whispers.

The summer went by in a haze of public-service manual labor, plus long, solitary runs and makeup work and correspondence courses he had to pass in order to be a junior come September. He was not unhappy to be changing schools, although he felt bad for his father. Many days, invisibility was his principal wish. He had to admit, though, that he did not want to be dead, not just yet.

Jake doesn't feel that he has learned much so far in his life, but one thing he knows: you can never get comfortable.

The school day goes by uneventfully until the very end, until after he's said goodbye to Andrea and promised to call her later.

He has picked up a civics book from his locker and is turning when he sees Pete Fallon standing behind him, waiting. Smirking.

"I heard you were laughin' at me," he says, stepping forward.

Jake tries to deny it. He's made a point of never talking about Pete Fallon at all.

"Bullshit," the other boy says, talking over him. "You think you can just walk in here and steal my girl? Do you?"

Jake knows anything he says now will be wrong, but his silence just seems to infuriate the other boy more.

"You and me," he says. "You and me. I'm gonna send your ass to the emergency room, I promise."

There are only a couple of other students near them, and Pete Fallon is speaking quietly. Jake can see that he is truly livid, not trying to save face or grandstand for his friends.

"I don't want to fight you."

"You don't want to fight me," Pete Fallon says in a falsetto voice. "You chickenshit. You're going to fight me. I'm not going to do it to you now, though. I'm going to wait until the last game is over, 'cuz I don't want to get kicked off the team for some loser, car-stealing faggot like you, unless I just can't help myself. But when I've played my last game . . ."

He draws a finger across his throat.

"In the meantime, though, I'm going to try to make your life a living hell."

The assistant principal has just turned the corner, fifty feet away. Pete Fallon waves to the man, who waves back. Then he walks away.

Jake has not fought since he was in second grade. He wonders what it will feel like to be beaten by the football team's most-feared player. When Andrea Cross, long-lost playmate from the old neighborhood, a girl he hadn't seen since they were eight years old, reappeared on his first day at Barton, and they somehow hit it off, he thought he could feel the dynamics of his world shifting, his luck changing. Now, though, as her thug ex-boyfriend swaggers away, he wonders if anything ever really changes.

Invisibility has seldom seemed so desirable.

CHAPTER FOUR

Jake asks his father again, while their guest is showering, exactly what Freeman Hawk did to merit his flight from Canada under an assumed name.

"Don't know all the details, but I can assure you it wasn't anything really bad. I'm pretty sure it's political. It's always been political with Freeman."

Jake is silent.

"Oh, Freeman's always been a little paranoid." The way George says it, looking away with a half-hearted shrug, does not reassure Jake.

He tells his father paranoia must be contagious.

On Jake's birthday, George and Carrie take him to dinner. He is allowed to invite Andrea as well. "Chris Rainier" does not join them but does give Jake a gift, a secondhand copy of *Johnny Got His Gun* that he bought at the Black Swan on one of his solitary walks.

"It's a pretty grown-up book," Freeman Hawk says. "I doubt they'll be teaching it in high school anytime soon."

Jake would have preferred to have gone somewhere like Bottoms Up Pizza or even the Five Guys burger place that has just opened three blocks away, but George thought a sixteenth birthday deserved something more grand.

Jake thinks that the person who most wanted to go to Morton's probably is George himself, who has not eaten red meat in three weeks. Certainly, Carrie does not seem happy with the choice, although at least she has made the effort.

Jake self-consciously opens gifts from his father (a gift certificate to Jos. A. Bank worth the price of a decent suit) and Carrie (tickets to a University of Virginia football game in November for him and his father).

Everything seems larger than life, even the waiters. A linebacker in a white jacket shows them all the enormous cuts of beef from which they can choose. They are advised that the "sides" are large enough for two or more to share. The linebacker even brings out a live lobster that weighs more than three pounds.

"If that lobster could talk," Andrea whispers to Jake, "he'd ask us to let him die with a little dignity."

Andrea seems completely up to the evening. She is dressed in a modest but elegant black dress from Ann Taylor. She has borrowed a string of her mother's pearls. Her red hair is so stunningly alive that its loose strands look like a solar storm radiating from her glowing face. He believes she could illuminate the room in lieu of electricity. She is so beautiful, so adult, that Jake, who feels like a child in his barely compatible tie and shirt and slightly rumpled sports jacket, can scarcely concentrate enough to order.

Andrea selects the smallest steak on the menu. Carrie goes with the salmon.

"At least," she says with a grimace, "I'm not *sure* they feel pain."

"We can always hope," George says. He orders a rib eye the size of his plate. Jake says he'll have the same.

The baked potatoes, when they come, are so huge that they're all speechless for a few seconds.

"Jesus," George says at last, "they must have grown those things downwind from Chernobyl."

Only George eats everything. Carrie asks Jake if she can try a bite of his steak when it's obvious he can't begin to finish it.

"Might as well go all the way," she says. "In for a salmon, in for a rib eye."

She eats at least a third of Jake's order with such poorly concealed gusto that she confirms what he has felt for some time—Carrie Bass shuns red meat for her health, not some animal's.

"She's gone from eschewing to chewing," George says.

They drop Andrea at her house. She hasn't given Jake a present yet. He walks her to her door, and when they kiss good night, she whispers, "I'll give you your present later. Promise." As she says it, she slides her hand down his tie and a few inches beyond, touching him lightly. He is glad for the darkness as he walks back to his father's car.

When they get back to Warwick, Carrie comes up with them for a few minutes and then leaves, saying she has to get up early the next morning.

She has not been staying over as often since Freeman Hawk arrived, although on three occasions over the past two weeks, George has come back from evenings at her place long after Jake went to bed. The last time, he woke Jake slipping in with the paper, sometime after 6. He apologized for waking him.

"You're grounded," Jake said, taking the sports section away. His father seemed relieved at what he hoped was humor.

Jake doesn't really know how to act. Carrie and George have been dating for six months now. She seems to adore him. She's about half his age and bears more than a passing resemblance to photos Jake has seen of his mother when she was in her twenties, something he has not mentioned but can't believe George doesn't realize.

Jake likes Carrie, or enjoys her company at least, but he has argued with his father about her, telling him he wishes he would slow down a little. George tells him over and over how she will never replace his mother, but Jake sometimes feels as if she is doing just that, step by step.

Jake is pleased that George has not revealed Chris Rainier's true identity to Carrie. He and his father share a secret.

It's a Friday night, and they stay up later than they normally would, talking. Jake appreciates that his father probably would rather be with Carrie right now, that this is a kind of birthday gift, too, so he tries to sustain his end of the conversation. Without Carter as a link, the two of them find talking difficult.

By the time Freeman Hawk comes back, sometime after midnight, the conversation has come around to colleges. With what George calls "the late unpleasantness" of last spring behind them, he still holds out hope that his son will become the shining academic star he once was and could be again. Jake knows that his grades, when they come out, will not make George happy, and he tries now to soften the blow by being deliberately ambiguous about his plans.

Freeman joins them in the living room just as George shrugs and repeats his mantra, "Well, there's always New Hope."

"Good God," Freeman murmurs.

"Aw, it was a fine school," George says, turning to his old friend. "We had a good education there."

"In spite of New Hope College. We educated ourselves."

"You educated yourself," George says. "Then you educated me. And you didn't even have to pay for it."

Freeman concedes the point.

"What was so wrong with New Hope?" Jake asks. He has no affinity for the school. In fact, he is inclined not to like it, if only because his father is constantly bringing it up as some kind of consolation prize. "I mean, it sounds like it was kind of neat."

Freeman Hawk rubs his bald head and allows himself a half-smile.

"We were all neat," he says. "And then some of us got kind of messy."

"You were never neat," George replies, yawning.

42

Because it's late and it's his birthday, Jake feels entitled to ask Freeman Hawk what exactly he is running from, why he is here.

"Long story," he says, giving Jake the kind of straight-on look he seldom gets from his father. "If I told you, I'd have to kill you, or at least maim you."

Jake stares him down.

"You're our guest," he says. "The least you can do is stop bullshitting me."

George tells him he's being rude, but Freeman Hawk smiles and shakes his head.

"Believe me, Jake, you're better off not knowing everything you want to know.

Their sophomore year, George James and Freeman Hawk saw each other now and again. It was always up to George to drop by the cinder-block off-campus apartment to which his old roommate had moved, one that seemed to have an ever-changing cast of residents. Freeman didn't feel comfortable going to the Sigma Nu house, and George was ashamed to admit to himself that he wasn't comfortable with him there.

The war ground on. A few more people now accompanied Freeman Hawk, his small band of student dissidents and the faculty wives. The only coffeehouse on campus was thriving. There seemed to be an endless supply of young men and women with average voices and marginal guitar and songwriting skills.

"Change is coming," Freeman would say again and again. Most of the students were only vaguely aware of any shift in their world's axis. This was the only campus life, the only semi-adult world they'd known. Whatever happened seemed normal. Even as change happened, George sensed that most of his classmates stumbled, as he did, from one spot to another—led by various appetites or self-preservation—rather than blazing a trail. Only Freeman acted as if he knew where he was going.

The campus went for Nixon by a slim margin in a mock election. (Most of them weren't old enough to vote in the real one.) The fraternity boys thought they heard him promise to go in there and "nuke the shit out of those gooks," as the Sigma Nu president said one night to great acclaim. The nascent New Hope left thought he was telling them, with a wink and a nod, that he'd find a way out of the jungle.

"People hear what they want to hear," Freeman said. He scorned Humphrey and traded his Eugene McCarthy pin for one bearing Ho Chi Minh's likeness after he, Andre, Tim Fairweather and the Scag Sisters went to Chicago for the Democratic convention and came back seemingly embarrassed that they had not managed to get beaten or even arrested.

George tried not to talk politics. He wanted it all to go away. He didn't like verbal conflict, which seemed to set him apart from Freeman and most of the war protesters who orbited around him. But George James was a good-natured nineteen-year-old who felt he should be loyal to all his friends, no matter now disparate their interests. And Freeman Hawk was worth knowing. He was, George thought, the brightest student he knew at New Hope, maybe the brightest person he'd ever known. He was already one of the stars of the student newspaper and seemed to have a hand in just about any campus organization that would have been defined as progressive. He was more interesting if a good deal more dangerous than the guys at Sigma Nu.

George had seen how, at the same time Freeman alienated almost anyone with money or the promise of future influence, he took it upon himself to befriend those who didn't quite fit in. Two of Freeman's most vicious enemies at New Hope would later go on to be governor and lieutenant governor of the state, while he seemed drawn to the nerds, the sexually or racially marginalized, the physically afflicted, as long as they were smart and fearless. George sensed that being out of the popularity pool encouraged such qualities.

"What do I have to lose?" Tim Fairweather asked once when George was over. "My standing with the Dekes and the other frat boys? Excuse me, George. My future in the old boy network? Unless I wake up in the morning craving pussy, I'm already so down I might as well be black. Excuse me, Andre."

They would argue occasionally. Freeman knew an amazing amount about the French in Vietnam, "Uncle Ho" and the failings of the standing Vietnamese government. That fall, though, even with the election raging, the debates lacked much venom on either side.

Then, in January of 1969, Sam Culbreth was killed, and there was a shift.

They'd known him in Satterwhite the year before. He was drafted after he graduated and was killed while they were home on Christmas break. George remembered Sam Culbreth as the guy who would flip the burgers at dorm cookouts, the guy who'd let freshmen crowd into his room so they could watch the Smothers Brothers' show rather than having to depend on the ancient TV in the basement. They'd all been amazed that Sam let himself get drafted. Nobody did that. You might go as an officer if you were ROTC, but any middle-class white college graduate could find an Army Reserve or National Guard unit somewhere.

"Do you think Sam ought to be allowed to die in vain?" George asked Freeman and four other students who had just come back from a peace rally at Duke sputtering their disdain for the American military. "He believed in fighting communism. And now we're just gonna say too bad, we were just kidding?"

Freeman usually let the others do most of the talking. This time, though, he cleared his throat a little, an almost inaudible sound. George was amazed at how the others, many of them older, automatically yielded the floor to him, despite the fact that they all were eager to verbally eviscerate this callow, callous fratty-bagger in their midst.

"I'm sorry, man, but he already has died in vain. Not a damn thing we can do about that. But don't you see, every time a Sam Culbreth or somebody else good and noble, with all the highest ideals, dies over there, it gets harder to bring the rest of 'em back. You lose one so you send two over to avenge his death, and they get killed, and you have to send four over because now we're *really* pissed, and then three of them die. It just goes on and on. You make a bad decision, then you make another worse decision to justify that one, just riding all those bad moves straight into hell."

George didn't really buy it. He was not without intelligence, but the rest of his world, away from Freeman Hawk and his crowd, was spent among people like his fraternity brothers, who never considered opposing a war they'd never see unless they went voluntarily, or like his father, who said he felt every generation had a duty to be in at least one damn good war.

"You never want to go to war," Wash James had told George when they talked about it over the summer, "but by God, sometimes you have to, and whatever doesn't kill you makes you tougher.

"Not," he'd said quickly, backtracking, "that there's any danger of you getting killed or anything. Hell, most college guys are probably a million miles from the shooting. Not like World War II."

George seemingly was born with a knack for staying cordial with almost everyone. He could listen to what the rest of the campus was calling Hawk's Doves, nod his head, make a point or two, then go back to the Zoo and manage not to offend his fraternity brothers with his unconventional (by their lights) view of Vietnam's merits.

But it was getting harder and harder to walk the tightrope. One winter day, one of the Doves spit on George, then seemed offended when George tried to get him to fight.

That spring, George only came by the mildewed home of Freeman Hawk at 105 Arbor Drive if there was little or no sign of other visitors. They saw each other on campus, had a beer together once in a while, but most of the people around Freeman had no ties to George James, no reason to think of him as anything except one more self-absorbed rich boy. (Plenty of those among the anti-war crowd also had chosen their parents well, Freeman once noted.)

In April, Freeman and another friend had to break up a fight between George and a boy who insisted on calling George a pig repeatedly and at close range. After that, he stayed away from the place on Arbor Drive.

The episode that would become known around New Hope as the Bay of Pigs took place the week before exams, too late to be chronicled in the yearbook, barely mentioned in the campus paper. Freeman, who by then had his own column, made an oblique reference to it, but he could only write so much without being thrown out of school.

The week before, a handful of boys from Sigma Nu broke up a candlelight anti-war vigil by pelting its participants with rotten eggs thrown from a passing pickup truck. No one was caught, but everyone seemed to know who did it.

George searched Freeman out after his 10 A.M. class the next day, and swore to him that neither he nor most of the house knew about the egging beforehand.

"Well," Freeman said, "are you going to turn them in, then?"

"You know I can't do that."

Freeman shrugged.

"Well, it'll take care of itself. Things have a way of evening up."

George thought Freeman was talking about something long-range, like karma.

The Sigma Nu house sat on a hill, its faux-antebellum columns overlooking a plain that was used for various intramural sports. On the other side of the field was a mini-mart that was the brothers' main source of beer.

Every Sigma Nu had to go through a rite of passage whose origin was lost in the haze of time and alcohol: at the end of his sophomore year, he had to run from the house to the mini-mart, buy a six-pack and run back up the hill. He had to make the run, some 200 yards each way, naked.

The date and time of the annual Sigma Nude run was the worst-kept secret on campus. It was not unusual for two or three hundred fellow students to be there on the appointed night, waiting under the lights at the convenience store. The time, as always, was midnight.

The afternoon of the Sigma Nude run, George got a call.

"This is just for you," the voice said. "One-time favor for an old friend. Don't do the run tonight. Hang back. Get sick or something."

"Freeman?"

The line went dead before George could ask anything else.

That night, George anesthetized himself the same way he did before blind dates or pickup forays in Greensboro bars.

By 11:55, he was into his second six-pack. He stripped down to his tennis shoes.

Then they were marching out to the edge of the hill. In the distance, across the intramural fields, they could see and hear their audience. Seconds before the starter's gun sounded, George stepped back and disappeared into the darkness.

"Gotta pee," he said to the hoots of his upper-class brothers.

The fields hadn't been used for a week. No one noticed the black figures who had slid down the wooded north bank of the plain at twilight, several hoses snaking behind them. No one saw them attach the hoses to sprinkler-system faucets and turn them on. It had been an unusually cool day, and no one else went down there between sundown and midnight.

The clay around New Hope makes excellent bricks and pottery. In 1969, the area already abounded in kilns. The same clay, when wet, became as slick as ice. Few freshmen from elsewhere failed to fall in spectacular fashion at least once before learning to tread lightly on rainy days.

By the time the whistle sounded, the field below had been saturated for more than five hours.

The first boys sprinted down the hill into the darkness to lusty cheers. They were well into the plain before they hit the first stretch of red muck. Some of them lost their only items of clothing when their shoes were sucked off their feet in the mud, and all of them fell. They tumbled over each other in the darkness. The shouts of confusion and consternation perplexed the brothers waiting atop the hill for their return, and some of them ventured into the mire and became enmeshed in the general chaos.

The pigs were released thirty seconds after the first boys descended.

They gravitated toward the natural hog wallow that the water and the thrashing boys had created. By the time the two searchlights attached to the trucks parked at the north end of the field were turned on, several dozen clothed and unclothed Sigma Nus were trying to get away from a half-dozen half-grown North Carolina pigs. One of the sophomores had to be rescued from three of the animals who seemed to have taken a liking to him. The crowd across the way near the convenience store, as confused as the Sigma Nus, eventually went away feeling well-entertained after watching the fraternity boys claw their way back up the hill from which they had descended, with several of the pigs trailing them, as the lights were extinguished. George slipped into the mire just enough to get some mud on himself and avert suspicion.

A farmer came in the morning to retrieve his pigs, which he claimed were taken by parties unknown the day before. George James had biked out into the country with Freeman

Hawk a couple of times to visit a cousin of Freeman's who lived in Charity. The cousin raised hogs.

"He's not too crazy about fraternity boys," Freeman said. "And he likes a good joke."

"So," Jake asks, "did anybody ever get caught?"

"No, not really. I mean, there were people who knew, but the administration probably saw it as a case of two stupids making one smart. They'd never liked the idea of their young gentlemen running around campus bare-assed, and the Bay of Pigs gave them an excuse to crack down on such 'unseemly behavior.'"

"But the Sigma Nu guys had a pretty good idea who did it," George adds. "And they knew I'd roomed with the infamous Freeman Hawk my freshman year. I don't think some of my brothers ever quite trusted me after that."

"Sorry about that. I broke some eggs back then."

"It worked out."

"So," George turns to his son, "The original Chris Rainier rid the campus of Old South days and Confederate flags, and this impostor here took care of the Sigma Nude run."

Freeman turns toward Jake.

"You asked me about what I'd done to get in such deep shit. Well, for want of a better answer, doing what you can will take you to some strange places, places you didn't mean to go."

CHAPTER FIVE

Coach Gage believes there is something ineffably noble about the pure, unadulterated act of running until everyone except you has surrendered to fatigue. It isn't about being fast, Coach Gage tells his charges every year. (This is fortunate, because Barton has never had a student who could break ten seconds in a 100-yard dash.)

"It is about pain," he tells them, sometimes squashing a cigarette with his shoe as he says it. "It is about staring pain in the face and saying, 'I don't care about you. You mean nothing to me.' "

He spent three hours over two separate meetings before he persuaded Jake to run for Barton. Jake was in good shape; he still enjoyed the long, silent runs around Byrd Park or through the streets of the Fan, runs in which he could lose himself briefly. He just didn't want to compete.

Jake does have talent, though. Anyone can see that. He's always been able to run just about forever. George kidded him that he must have gotten it from some of their ancestors who stayed alive only by being able to outrun the gentiles.

In his only cross-country meet so far, a four-school event, he finished second.

Today, he feels sluggish in the early going. He almost trips once on the trail that takes them through suburban woods. He considers quitting. Almost always, he is able to overcome the early feeling of hopelessness, and today is no exception.

He is almost sprinting at the end, surprised with the burst of energy he never expects to have but usually does. He passes the last boy from Trinity fifty yards from the end and is a good four steps in front at the finish line.

Easing into a winded walk, just before he turns back to be congratulated by his teammates, he is off his feet, sliding face-first along the damp grass, before he even knows he's been hit.

"Better watch where you're going, dipshit," Pete Fallon says, then walks away, flanked by three of his teammates, before anyone can do anything. "Why don't you come out for football?" he says over his shoulder. "I'll show you how to play a real sport."

Andrea has followed Jake past the finish line. Now she runs up and hits her former boyfriend from behind. He almost falls over, then turns and seems momentarily chagrined to see her there.

Then he regains his swagger.

"If you ever get tired of second-best," he says, working up his best sneer, "I might take you back."

"Thanks for the offer," Andrea says, facing down Pete Fallon and his three friends, "but you're just not man enough for me, pencil dick."

She puts her arm around Jake, who is now upright if a bit dazed, and walks him back toward the finish line. He knows he should go back and do something pyrrhic regarding Pete Fallon, but he is happy just to be led away. He would do almost anything to avoid a fight, but he feels as if he would descend into the lions' den for Andrea Cross right now.

"You OK, son?" Coach Gage asks, looking back to see how the rest of his team is faring. He didn't seem to see any of it, and neither did most of Jake's teammates. "Take a tumble?"

"Yes, sir."

"Well, brush yourself off. I'll bet you're glad I talked you into running now."

"Yes, sir."

Actually, all Jake has wanted for some time now is to disappear. Having the meanest guy on the football team as his avowed enemy just makes him want it more.

He accepts his new teammates' congratulations, and then Andrea leads him away.

"I guess Pete thinks we're screwing. I hope he thinks that. WUH-gaf," she says when they reach her car. Jake has not gotten used to the casual way in which Andrea refers to almost any bodily function.

Most of Andrea's verbal text-message acronyms seem to have what his father still calls the F-word in them. WGAF (WUH-gaf) means "Who gives a fuck?" IFDI ("if die") is "I fucking doubt it." FMD (she just uses the initials for that one) means "Fuck me dead," a term that seems to take in a variety of emotions from amazement to exasperation to despair.

"Don't you care about my reputation?" Jake asks, grinning. "What will people think?"

Andrea laughs and begins to tickle him. He tickles her back, and soon they are making out in her car, right there in the dirt parking lot next to the course. He has gotten beneath her bra before. Today, for the first time, she does not try to stop his other hand as it slides up her thigh.

"Aren't you afraid of getting caught?" she asks. She is stroking him, too, through his sweaty running shorts.

He can only moan and finally slide his hand inside the fabric of her panties. He has only gotten this far with one girl, a freshman he dated several times in the magnet school. She disappeared like most of his former friends, although he never made much effort, either. The ones he didn't lose after his leap from the pedestrian bridge seemed to stop calling after his arrest.

Jake knows he should make a serious effort to go further, and he makes a half-hearted attempt to get Andrea to come with him to a more secluded area in a park nearby.

"Let's just do this for now," she murmurs, and he is willing to settle for that. More than willing, really.

Andrea drops him off at the Warwick. Her scent will linger with him for the rest of the day.

He lets himself in through the second set of doors with his fob. As he goes inside, he is met by Melody Carrington, who is making her way in his direction, right hand firmly on the rail that was added when one elderly resident fell in the lobby and broke her hip. He opens the door for her and stands there for five minutes, even though he's dying to get upstairs and take a shower, as she asks him in great detail about his day. She, like all his Warwick aunts, seems genuinely interested in his activities.

"First place," she says, beaming. "Well, that's just wonderful. It's just a shame you're too late to make the Olympics this time. Well, four years isn't that far away."

He can tell that she's kidding him. When they first moved, the residents would sometimes catch him off-guard with their dry wit. They don't remind him of the older relatives he remembers. He has learned that they demand his respect. He cannot humor them or condescend to them. Half the time, he isn't sure whether they're having fun at his expense or not.

As she is leaving, she turns back.

"Oh, have you or your father noticed that man in the park?"

Jake shakes his head. "What man?"

"Oh, maybe I can see him better. He's just hanging around there. I watched him yesterday, and he didn't move for it seemed like three hours. I thought about calling the police."

Jake notes that he has seen many people in the park fail to move for so long he thought they might be dead.

"But this one," she says, "this one seems to be killing time on purpose. He'll sit down and lean against one of the oaks, and then, when one of the folks that stay there comes up to him, he'll look up and it seems like he's talking to them, and they go away like he's scared them or something.

"Then he'll get up and go sit down by some other tree. I got my high-powered binoculars out the other day. He had on nice slacks and a dress shirt, and they looked like they'd been pressed. And he was reading a book. Who in that park, other than the students, has ever been seen reading a book?"

Jake nods politely. He doesn't really care if the intellectual quality of street life below him is improving. Melody Carrington is a smart woman. He'll concede that. But she might have too much time on her hands up there on the eleventh floor.

"Say hi to your dad," Melody says as she leaves. "And bring your aunt by. I'd love to meet her."

Jake nods. Tyler James is coming up from Mexico tomorrow to sign some papers and help George bring the sale of Old Dominion Country Hams one step further toward reality.

Jake walks into the apartment and finds Freeman Hawk there alone.

"Your dad had a meeting, probably about selling his hogs," Freeman says with a small smile. "Said he'd be back sometime soon."

Jake sees that Freeman has been looking through the bookcase. He has settled on the history of the family company, the one Jake's grandfather paid a local novelist to write in 1989.

"Best paycheck he ever got," Wash loved to say at the club.

"This is fascinating stuff," Freeman says. "You know, I'd known your father for a year probably before he told he was more or less Jewish."

"More or less."

Some of Jake's friends were given Old Testament first names with no family precedent. His classes have had their share of Noahs, Daniels, Naomis and Josephs. "Jacob" by itself would have just been going with the serious, substantial, Before Christ trend. Jacob Malachi James, though, required an explanation, at least in Richmond.

"You have something to be proud of," his mother explained. "You have a heritage. You have history."

Who, he wondered silently, wanted history?

The first James to come to Richmond, Malachi Jacobsen, moved there in 1866. He had been a boy when he and his family came over from Prussia, and he had seen little outside his ghetto existence in New York City until he was drafted into the Civil War. He first saw Virginia in the reluctant, immigrant-heavy ranks of an invading army. He first saw Richmond in smoldering ruins after the siege of Petersburg succeeded and ended a year of misery and terror.

He was a carpetbagger and made no excuses for it. He figured if those bastards south of the Potomac, the ones who killed his two best friends, had caused him this much distress, they owed him a new life, any kind of life other than what he saw in New York City, where immigrants' dreams were like lottery tickets.

Malachi Jacobsen was not religious. His parents had tried, but preserving his identity was a casualty in the sheer, basic fight for survival. It was not profitable to be a Jew in Richmond, or at least not a Jewish immigrant from Up North.

He married into a lower-class gentile family, and he named his ninth and last child George Washington James. (Mal James took his adopted family name from the river two blocks down from the store where he first clerked and which he later bought.)

The first George Washington James would be called G.W. The second one was Wash. The Jameses eventually became wealthy in the selling and then exporting of Virginia hams, something about which none of them ever seemed to suffer pangs of conscience.

G.W. served twelve years in the Virginia General Assembly, and it seemed obvious to him that his only son, Wash, would take the dream one step farther.

George Washington James II was born in 1924. In timing and temperament, he was perfectly positioned, after World War II, to make Old Dominion Country Hams truly worldwide.

Wash James was, everyone agreed, something of what his old college friends from the University of Virginia and his buddies at the club called a bullshit artist. They all liked him, and if he wanted to embellish a little here or there, what was the harm?

G.W. thought the next chapter of the dream was obvious: his son would be governor, even senator. Hell, who knew how far he could go? He had name recognition, charm, the right school, the right club, plenty of money.

It might have worked out that way. The path was paved. While his son was in college, Wash got himself elected to the General Assembly. He was past forty, but everyone agreed he was just a late bloomer. When the Democrats needed a candidate for lieutenant governor two years after George graduated, Wash James, still in his forties, got the nomination with a minimum of opposition. His campaign manager remarked that if he could keep from screwing sheep on the capitol steps for the next four years, he would be the odds-on favorite to be governor of Virginia in 1977.

George watched the wheels fall off Wash's campaign in early August. That's when an enterprising *Washington Post* reporter, acting on an anonymous tip, discovered that George Washington James II had not in reality seen "action" in World War II, much less been the nominal war hero his campaign implied he was. Wash James' action had consisted of leaving college in late 1944 to join the Army Air Corps, in whose ranks he never got beyond the confines of Pope Field in the safe, balmy pines of North Carolina. Everyone wondered how the canard of Wash James' bogus war exploits could have passed unchallenged as long as it did. There was a lot of talk along the lines of, "Hell, I knew ol' Wash was blowing smoke about some of it, but that's just how he was, you know?"

The most damning thing, the symbol that nailed Wash James and doomed his political ambitions, was the Purple Heart. He sometimes wore it rather conspicuously on Veterans Day or Memorial Day or the Fourth of July. He was described in flyers and TV ads as "a man who was willing to shed his blood for state and country," but, faced with the inescapable facts, Wash had to explain that the Purple Heart was a gift. An employee, whom Wash James had kept on the payroll long after his multiple sclerosis made it impossible for him to work, gave him the medal, which he'd earned during the Battle of the Bulge, to thank him for his kindness.

"You probably should have got one of these anyhow," the man had said, for he believed the stories Wash James told, as many people did.

After his fall, Wash James did not fade away. He would live another twenty-six years, and he still had his friends and his club and his money. He and Clara receded a little from public view. (For Clara, it was something of a relief. Her life was perfect before politics, she told a friend. How was politics going to make it better?)

George Washington James III was twenty-four and his sister, Tyler, was seventeen the year of the failed run for lieutenant governor. By then, George had made it clear that he was not going to be on the same career track as his father.

The two of them had never shared much except blood. George blames himself mostly for what he still considers the ultimate betrayal of his own beliefs, but Wash's role in it was an irreparable wound. Wash James won their private battle, in the summer of 1971, but when it came to his son, he lost the war.

"Hell," George said to Carter, more than once, "we both lost. They should have given us both purple hearts."

58

When George and Carter decided to name their only living child for George's long-ago wandering-Jew ancestor, after 133 years of whitewash, it might have been out of superstition. George Washington James IV, more than two months premature and damaged beyond repair, had lived for only four days. This time, George seemed to be saying, let's try the opposite of Roman-numeraled aristocracy.

Or it might have been a less-than-subtle barb aimed at Wash James' thick skin. It seemed to irritate George that his father truly did not seem to care what they named his first surviving grandson, as long as he was not damaged. It would be George's only bow toward his Jewish ancestry. The Jameses were, as they had been for more than a century, upstanding members of St. Paul's Episcopal.

Jake wonders why the name matters to his father, since Malachi Jacobsen obviously didn't want it. He doesn't really chafe about it, though. He has decided he would as soon be named for his great-great grandfather and the family pro-genitor as for George Washington. He does occasionally, though, yearn for something with no weight or expectations whatsoever.

"Can't believe George's dad could get away with that shit as long as he did," Freeman says, "but he was a charmer. I remember that. And people believe what they want to believe, not what they see right in front of them.

"Otherwise, how is that chimp about to be re-elected president?"

He doesn't say it with any venom, unlike George, who rants about the current president all the time, then shrugs his shoulders as if to say, What can you do?

Until now, Jake hasn't heard Freeman say anything about the president.

"I guess you probably really hate him," he says.

Freeman looks down and shakes his head.

"Nah. I'm not entitled. You know, if you don't like the club, you quit the club. But then you can't stand there throwing brickbats like you're still a dues-paying member."

"Then what are you doing back here?"

Freeman gives him a very thin smile.

"Just passin' through. One day you'll look out your window, and I'll be gone."

"I won't even think twice."

Freeman smiles a little wider.

"Any kid that knows his Dylan has got to be OK."

"That reminds me," Jake says, "the lady who lives up on the eleventh floor said something about some guy hanging out in the park, looking suspicious."

"Looks to me as if everybody on the East Coast without a place to stay hangs out in that park. Richmond must be a very accommodating town. How do you get to be suspicious among that crowd?"

"Mrs. Carrington said he looked too neat to be a bum. And he was reading a book."

Freeman frowns.

"Yeah, that's unusual, in that crowd, but people do read books, even homeless people. Sure he wasn't just using the pages for toilet paper? Huh."

He walks over near the window. Jake watches as he kneels and closes the matchstick blinds enough so that he can barely peek out through the slits.

"Can't see anybody like that now," he says. "If you do, will you tell me? Probably nothing."

But he looks worried, and the way he's acting worries Jake.

"What's the matter?"

"Nothing. I've been through worse than this. I'm just a little spooked is all. I just don't like being fucked with. Hell, I need to disappear for a couple of days anyhow, with your aunt coming and all."

He tells Jake about his first year in Canada, about getting beaten up several times as a suspected homosexual, hippie drug addict and deserter. He was part of the generally unwanted, pain-in-the-ass contingent trying to live in a foreign country with few skills that conveyed beyond their hometowns.

"It was probably better for me than some," he says. "I could speak some French, so I went to Montreal. I lived in the French part of the city, where there weren't many other American kids to give us a bad name. But it was bad enough, even so."

He shows Jake the scar on his head from thirty-two years ago, left by a Molson Ale bottle.

"Didn't even see it coming. I woke up two hours later, alone in this alley. I knew it was a Molson because parts of it were lying beside me when I came to."

For lack of a better war story, Jake tells him about Pete Fallon.

"So he just blind-sided you at the end of the race, and nobody did anything?"

"I don't think anybody much saw him. The coach didn't. I'm pretty sure of that."

Freeman is quiet for a moment.

"You know," he says finally, "everybody always just assumed that because I'd left the country to keep from going to Vietnam, that anybody could just fuck me over any way they wanted to. And I let 'em, for a while. I never did settle things with the guy who brained me with that bottle, never found out who it was.

"But a few months after that, these three tough Quebecois rednecks started hassling me in a bar. I don't think they knew I spoke French fluently, and it set 'em back for a few seconds when I said a few choice things about their mothers and sisters, in their native tongue.

"Then, before they could make a move, I leaned down like I was going to tie my shoes or something, and I came up like this"—he comes up toward Jake with his hands together, side by side, palm-up—"and I caught one of them under the chin. Knocked him out cold. My father taught me that trick, about the only thing he ever seemed capable of teaching me, other than to hide when he was drinking. I kicked the bigger of the other two in the nuts, then caught him under the chin, too. The third guy, he just left."

Freeman Hawk pauses, as if he's said more than he meant to.

"The point is," he says, "I'd been fighting all along, just to feed myself and stay solvent in a foreign country. I thought it was a good time to let somebody know that being against an unjust war didn't necessarily mean you were Gandhi."

"Maybe I ought to try that move on Pete Fallon."

Freeman shakes his head.

"No, wait now. Don't necessarily do what I did. I put up with a bunch of crap a lot of times. I didn't fight every time somebody wanted me to. Besides, I was probably twenty-three years old by then. It's easier to get yourself in a blind rage at twenty-three than it is at sixteen. You become less forgiving of fools."

Jake feels as if he's fairly unforgiving right now. He goes to bed fantasizing about ways to make Pete Fallon beg for mercy, none of which seem to have much basis in reality.

CHAPTER SIX

Everyone knew Tyler lived in Oaxaca, had never married and shared a villa with her friend Maria. Nobody talked about it. Back at George and Carter's home the day of Wash's funeral five years ago, Tyler stood up on a chair and announced to a rather large gathering of friends and their dwindling family that she and Maria had been "married" for five years.

"Not in Virginia, you ain't," Jake, who was eleven, overheard an old acquaintance of Wash's mutter behind him. He looked over at his father, who looked as if he wanted to become invisible or deaf.

"Jesus," George said to his sister later, when the crowd had cleared, "couldn't you wait a while?"

"I'm forty-three years old," she said as she took another sip of bourbon. "I think I've waited long enough."

Jake, not knowing what else to do and falling back on manners, shook both their hands and congratulated them.

GEORGE AND his sister get along well enough. He seems uncomfortable when she and Maria get overly affectionate, but he tries to hide it.

Although she and Maria offered to stay and are staying at the Radisson down the street, Freeman Hawk has disappeared, leaving enough of his gear behind to assure George and Jake that he will be back.

"So," Tyler asks, "what's it going to feel like, being filthy rich?"

George frowns, then smiles without much enthusiasm. "Well, maybe not filthy. Maybe just a little soiled."

Tyler has done reasonably well as an artist, better than George ever would have thought. He never discouraged her, but he never really believed he'd see his little sister's work exhibited in Washington and New York.

"Aren't you afraid all that easy money will ruin your creativity?" he asks her.

"Aren't you afraid it'll destroy your vaunted work ethic?"

He gives a short laugh. "I guess we'll just have to go to hell together."

"More interesting people there."

Tyler and Maria sometimes converse in Spanish. His aunt seems to have forgotten how fluent Jake has become in her adopted language, and he doesn't remind her until today, her first full day in Richmond since she left after Carter's funeral.

She tells Maria her nephew looks so much like his mother, especially the eyes.

"Thank you," Jake says in Spanish. "And you resemble your mother, as well."

Tyler and Maria have said a few things to each other in Spanish that were less than complimentary of George, the city of Richmond and the United States, in addition to exchanging a few endearments of a purely sexual nature; but they seem only momentarily taken aback.

"So you understand everything we're saying?"

"Pretty much," Jake says, blushing a little and furious with himself for doing it. Is he ever going to be an adult?

"Well, you little stinker." His aunt rubs his hair and laughs.

"Very bad boy," Maria says, smiling.

Tyler was there at the end. She flew up on a Wednesday, and Carter died on Friday. She didn't go back for a week afterward and felt guilty for not staying longer. She was serious when she told Jake he could come to Oaxaca to visit any time he wanted, but she was surprised when he called her from the airport last December, almost a year later.

"You really do look like her," Tyler says, now smoothing her nephew's hair. "And you have her disposition, too. She did some pretty wild stuff when she was young, too, things I'll bet your dad didn't tell you about. But you always knew somehow she'd get past it. Not a mean bone in her body. I was four years younger than she was, but she never made me feel like some jerky little kid, which I was."

"What did she do? That was so wild, I mean."

Tyler looks toward Maria as if seeking permission to tell it. George is napping, something he never did until the last year.

"Well, I guess you know she got kicked out of St. Catherine's. I mean, they let her back in the next year, but . . ."

"She got kicked out of St. Catherine's?" Tyler might as well have told him his mother was a devil-worshiper. Four generations of Bessette women had graduated from St. Catherine's. "What . . . what for?"

"Shoplifting. Three of them went to Miller and Rhoads, just on a lark or a dare or something. They caught Carter with, I think, a pair of earrings in her purse."

"Why didn't anybody tell me?" Jake knew his mother as the model of decorum. She was the "cool mom" who would teach him how to dance and try to understand his music, but she could keep a van full of rowdy nine-year-old soccer boys under control without ever raising her voice.

"Well, it was embarrassing, I guess. She probably didn't want you to think of her as some kind of bad example or something, and George probably didn't think you ought to know anything uncomplimentary about your mom. And I probably shouldn't have told you. Don't let him know you know. To me, though, it just makes . . . made . . . her human."

Others have tried to excuse Jake's self-destructive behavior as a way of lashing out at the mother who was cruel enough to die when he was only fourteen. Most of his shame for his actions is caused by her unseen presence.

He can't forget that last day, when he, his father and Tyler were led too courteously into a conference room by one of the doctors, a grief counselor and a nurse, and told that Carter Bessette James could not be saved. They seemed to Jake to be slightly impatient, as if his mother was taking up valuable space that could be occupied by some other no-hoper.

She and George had living wills, and the three of them agreed that she wouldn't want to suffer, although no one could tell whether she was suffering or not. The leukemia caused by the chemotherapy that was supposed to kill the breast cancer came on so fast that Jake refused to admit he was losing her until that conference.

They went back out and stood on each side of Carter. George stroked her forehead. Jake hesitated, then put his hand on her left shoulder . He could not make himself look at her for more than a second at a time. She did not resemble herself from even a week ago. She was swollen, with tubes everywhere hooked to the now-silent machines and their cruel, indisputable numbers. Jake is fairly certain she did not hear his last, choked "Love you, Mom."

And then, she was gone.

They got through the next three days on adrenaline. After that, they were alone. Jake never realized how little he and his father really talked until Carter died.

Half an hour later, George comes out of the bedroom, wiping sleep from his eyes.

"You didn't tell me he understood Spanish," his sister says.

"Yeah," George says, yawning. "He's taking notes. I'll find out what you really said about me after you leave."

They talk about the sale, although George says he'd rather just "let it happen, not jinx it." Tyler says it should make them rich enough to survive at least a couple of generations of complete idleness. She tells George and Jake for the first time that she and Maria are hoping to adopt a child.

"Lucky kid," George says, and Tyler looks at him to make sure he's not being snide.

"What do you think Wash would have said about this? I mean, us selling everything the sainted ancestors suffered and bled and died for?"

"Probably spinning like a top over in Hollywood Cemetery."

"Hell," Tyler says, "I've already made him rotate. Maria and I."

"Well, he'll get over it. It won't kill him."

They laugh and have another drink.

Jake knows George, despite his jokes about it, is not totally sanguine about divorcing the James family from the company. It was he, after all, who chose to preserve Malachi Jacobsen's name by giving it to his only living son.

"We don't have much choice, though," he says, as he's said many times before, as if trying to convince himself. "The time is right. And Jake here doesn't want to be the ham king, do you?"

Jake shakes his head, the way he always does. Any great love the James family had for Old Dominion Country Hams or pigs in general died with Wash. George has merely endured it. Being the CEO of a ham company was not hard labor, and he accepted it as his rather comfortable fate. Jake, George feels sure, would not go so far as to even endure it.

"When's your friend coming back? Free Bird or whatever."

George has told Tyler his real name and the barest of details, swearing her to secrecy, knowing she'll be back in Oaxaca soon.

"As soon as you get your ass out of here," he says. "Hell, you've met him, although you might not recognize him now. You came up the spring of my senior year, remember? After I moved out of the Sigma Nu house?"

"That guy? Jeez, yeah, I remember. Freeman Hawk and his doves. Talk about spinning. Old Wash looked like a roulette wheel when I told him I'd gone to see you for the weekend and had met your new roommate and all his friends."

After the Bay of Pigs, George didn't see or hear from Freeman Hawk for quite a while. He would read his stories and columns in the student paper, although Freeman had to resign in October of their junior year because he was making too much news to be allowed to comment on it.

The war protests in front of the post office had grown. They had moved it across the street to the edge of the campus, because they needed more room. There were three or four hundred there now, and it wasn't just one day. Every day from noon until 1 they protested. The silent, patient women who had started it all were no longer there, although Freeman tried to persuade them to stay.

"We primed the pump," one of them told him. "You can keep it going now."

George would see him walking across campus, but he tried to avoid running into him. Most of his fraternity brothers knew who instigated the Bay of Pigs, and he resented the distrust Freeman had sowed among the Zoo residents who knew they'd once been roommates.

They didn't speak more than twice their whole junior year, and by the fall of 1970, George had so immersed himself in the life of Sigma Nu that most of the others there didn't even remember that he'd once been a good friend of the student who was featured in his former newspaper as "the most dangerous man at New Hope."

Freeman somehow managed to keep his near-perfect grade-point average while being the ubiquitous center of the campus anti-war movement. He always wore a denim jacket and blue jeans. His hair was not unnaturally or even fashionably long for the times. He always seemed to be in a hurry, late for a class or a rally. It was his eyes, everyone agreed, that got you. He looked as if he could see what kind of underwear you had on, George's date said one night when a group of them were discussing Freeman Hawk.

"Hey," one of the younger brothers asked George, too loudly, "didn't I hear you used to be like roommates or something with that prick?"

George just stared at him until the boy looked away.

The two people who led George temporarily back into Freeman Hawk's orbit were Julia Weingarten and Tim Fairweather.

Julia was a sophomore. Everyone agreed that she was one of the most beautiful women on campus. She had long black hair, a perfect body and the kind of large, soulful brown eyes that would have stood her well without any other noteworthy enticements. Even George James, a relatively big man on the New Hope campus, hesitated to ask her out the fall of his senior year. He was a little surprised that she said yes.

They dated all that fall and winter. By November, they were sleeping together. She was Jewish and already had told him her father would never let her marry outside her religion, but George didn't care. He told her about his family's past and half-joked, "Maybe I'll go back." Somehow, it would work out. Besides, he couldn't let her go.

One day that winter, when he picked Julia up at her dorm to go to a Friday night party at the Zoo, she came downstairs wearing a black headband.

"I just went to the coolest thing," she said. "You know the peace rallies they have down on the green?"

She quickly became more and more involved in what she referred to as "the movement." A week later, George finally told her that he had once roomed with the charismatic figure who stood on the base of the Civil War monument and rallied his ragged, peaceful army, looking like some *sans-culotte* manning the barricades. He thought the information might impress her.

"You *know* Freeman Hawk?" she said.

"Well, we don't see much of each other anymore."

A week later, she came back and told George she had met him.

"He said to say hi," she said. "He wanted me to tell you he was sorry about the, um, Day of Pigs?"

"Bay of Pigs. Long story."

No more than two weeks later, she brought George up to her room (New Hope had incurred the wrath of many parents by going with more or less full visitation in some of the women's dorms), and there he was.

"Surprise," Julia said, obviously pleased with herself.

Looking at Freeman Hawk, George was struck by how much his beloved was styling herself after his old roommate. She could get by with wearing thrift-shop clothes; she was that beautiful. She could have chosen just about any item of clothing and half the girls at New Hope would have followed suit, assuming that they'd look hot in hand-me-downs, too.

They spent a couple of hours talking, with Julia mostly listening. She was an excellent listener who could make anyone feel special without contributing anything to the conversation beyond, "wow, that's amazing" or "and then what happened?"

She thought the Bay of Pigs story was just about the funniest thing she'd ever heard, even if George and his fraternity brothers were the butt of the joke. Even George could laugh about it by now.

Urged on by Julia, he went to a couple of the rallies. By now, almost everyone on campus seemed to be against the war, even some of the fraternity boys.

George knew he had a tendency to be easily influenced. He always told himself, when he joined Sigma Nu, that he would preserve his own identity, that he would never be like the guys who sat up on the roof sunning, making crude comments to the coeds walking by below, belittling anyone who appeared to be unhip and telling nigger jokes.

Reconnecting with his old friend was unsettling. Freeman Hawk was harder, colder, much more adult than when George knew him before. And George could see, through Freeman's eyes, how much he had been changed, too, by three years in a fraternity.

George thought later, when he had time to think, that he was balancing on the edge of a razor blade that winter and spring. The slightest breeze could have blown him either way.

It was his last semester, and he had been a good enough student. He wasn't brilliant, but he had amassed enough hours that he needed only nine to finish, and it didn't matter what they were.

George skated home to his degree by taking an advanced phys ed course designed for football players, beginning anthropology and a course in North Carolina history. Wash was not fully aware that his son was so slightly occupied, or if he was, he saw it as George's reward for finally hewing to the life course that had been designed for him. Many of Wash's friends had not been so lucky with their offspring. It was a troublesome time, they all agreed.

George's regimen left him a lot of freedom, and he found himself more and more, that early spring of 1971, drawn to his old friend Freeman Hawk. It was a source of some irritation at the Sigma Nu house, but George was a senior, an officer. He was allowed some leeway.

One day in early March, a day when the temperature rose into the mid-seventies and teased everyone into thinking spring had arrived, George was persuaded to cut his 1 o'clock anthro class and go to a bar favored by his fraternity. There were six of them, and they didn't leave until sometime after 9 that night, when one of the sophomores threw up on the table.

One of the attractions of the Dog House was that it was only a quarter-mile from the fraternity. It was difficult, someone had pointed out, to be arrested just for drunk walking.

They were a block up the street when a figure merged onto the sidewalk in front of them from a campus path, heading in the same direction as they were.

"Hey," one of the brothers said, "it's Fairy-weather!"

Most of the gays on the New Hope campus were cautious enough to keep a low profile. It was understood that they were not allowed to be at the forefront of something that might further offend the status quo. One strike was all they were allowed. Tolerance, after all, had its limits.

Tim Fairweather was either dumb or fearless. He was second only to Freeman Hawk in his visibility at rallies. With an effeminate manner that many thought was so beyond the pale that it must be for effect, he enraged the red-meat and Budweiser boys, the frat men who saw the late sixties (it was now 1971, but change came slowly to southern liberal-arts schools) as another Lost Cause to be contested heroically if vainly. At least two of those in the crowd of drunken Friday-nighters that assembled around Tim Fairweather had been in the last Old South parade two years earlier. They did not embrace change, especially if it discomfited them.

George did not dislike Tim Fairweather. He found him to be funny, self-deprecating and decent. In the time he'd spent around Freeman's friends, Hawk's Doves, he'd come to respect him. He knew he'd never have the courage to be so openly, unabashedly different. It would have been easier, George knew, to be Freeman Hawk than to be Tim Fairweather.

He had hoped that he might graduate from New Hope without ever having quite the cultural and moral conflict that was now facing him.

They surrounded Tim Fairweather and started gradually closing in, taunts turning to slaps. Standing at the back of the crowd and looking away, George hoped that their victim hadn't seen him. He told himself later that, if he hadn't been so drunk, he might have stepped in and done the right thing. But he didn't. George slipped away unnoticed and walked, not fast enough to attract attention, back toward the strip. There, ten minutes later, he finally flagged down a police car.

When he and the cop got back to the scene of the crime, Tim Fairweather was sitting there on the stone wall, nursing a bloody nose. His face looked puffy from the slaps and from crying. His clothes were torn and dirty. After a few seconds, George recognized the smell as the cop exclaimed "Damn!" They had thrown Fairweather to the ground, after they were through bullying him, and urinated on him.

The cop didn't seem to be overly sympathetic. He wound up calling one of the campus policemen, who offered to take Tim Fairweather to the hospital, but when he refused to identify his attackers, the campus cop finally shrugged and said, "Suit yourself," then got back into one of the golf carts they used to make New Hope seem more gentle than it really was, and rode away.

"How did you know I was here?" Fairweather asked.

"I saw them beating you up," George said after a couple of seconds, "and I went to get help."

Tim Fairweather looked at him, and George could see a moment of doubt, but then he said, "Well, thanks. I really appreciate somebody looking out for an old queer like me."

George told him to wait there, in the bushes, so as not to attract attention. He left and came back with his car and, trying not to think about the upholstery, drove Tim Fairweather home.

Two days later, George moved into Freeman Hawk's apartment, sharing his bedroom after he'd found a single bed frame and mattress for sale at the off-campus thrift shop. Even then, he didn't really confront anyone at the

Sigma Nu house about what happened to Tim Fairweather. He just let them figure it out on their own.

He did tell Freeman Hawk about that night. At first, he just told him the same story he'd told Tim, but he could see that Freeman didn't believe it, and he admitted his passive complicity, first making his old friend swear not to tell anyone else, especially Tim himself.

"Everybody does something once in a while that he's not proud of," Freeman said. "The trouble is, almost nobody ever admits it."

George made more of an impression his last ten weeks at New Hope than he had in the almost four years before. He managed to offend his former fraternity brothers to the point that (he learned years later) every one of them went into the 1971 school yearbook and cut his picture out of the fraternity "team photo." It hurt him to pass them on campus and see them either move away from him or just flat-out call him a commie or a traitor or a queer. He had to steel himself every day before leaving for class. (He was fortunate, he felt, that most of the classes were of such a dubious nature that his attendance was more or less optional.)

George was there every day at the peace demonstrations, and at every other campus protest or vigil, as if to catch up.

He lost a lot. Among other things, he lost Julia Weingarten, whose allegiances and attention span turned out to be somewhat tenuous. George didn't quit the Sigma Nus and move in with Freeman Hawk because of Julia, but when he thought about her the day he moved out, he thought it couldn't hurt.

"You mean," she said, "you just left, without saying anything? How about your friends? I mean, some of those guys seemed pretty neat. Like guys you'd be friends with your whole life, you know?"

It turned out that Julia Weingarten was in the process of deciding that life on fraternity and sorority row (she herself was a sorority girl, in one of the more radical ones that actually admitted a few Jews) was more interesting and worthwhile than anything Freeman Hawk and his doves had to offer. Within two weeks of George's desertion, she was dating one of the Sigma Nus, a fact his old frat brothers flaunted with great relish.

Wash James heard about it all a couple of weeks after George walked out. He drove down to New Hope and took his son to dinner at the local country club. Wash worried that his son's unkempt appearance (he made him put a sports jacket over his tie-dyed T-shirt) would reflect badly on him, but looking around the room that day, he saw that there were at least six other fathers there with student sons who appeared to be even more sullen and unwashed than his.

He threatened to take him back home "right damn now," but George called his bluff for once.

"I don't have to get a degree," he said. "You mess with me now, this close to graduation, I swear to God I'll just drop out."

Wash James retreated and waited for a better day.

CHAPTER SEVEN

Freeman Hawk returned the day after they put Tyler and Maria on the plane headed south. Tyler kissed her brother and nephew goodbye and made Jake promise to come for a long visit.

"This time," she said, holding Maria's hand, "you can stay forever. Just let us know you're coming first."

Jake asks Freeman where he went the bulk of the week.

"That place down the street. The Daily Planet?"

"You were in a homeless shelter?" George says. "Hell, I'd have put you up in a hotel. You didn't have to leave at all, for that matter."

"I just wanted to do it, you know? Three, four times up in Montreal, I did it just for the experience. It's kind of humbling. Although, I've gotta say, it is not an old fart's game. They make those beds uncomfortable enough that you want to get a job."

George frowns when Freeman scratches himself.

They are watching the news on CNN. A bomb has gone off in Iraq. Several members of a family have been killed. On the video, others weep and tear at their clothes.

"One of ours," Freeman Hawk mutters. "Way to win those hearts and minds. World War II didn't take much longer than this. Bush is never going to get out of this shit."

THE MORNING of September 11, 2001, George had been at the office, in a meeting, when a secretary came in and informed them all that an airplane had hit "one of those towers in New York City." George assumed it was some kind of small aircraft. He remembered photos he'd seen of one that had somehow managed to impale itself into the side of the Empire State Building during World War II.

There was a television in the room. All the executives sat there and watched, transfixed and helpless.

"It's the end," one of them, an MBA type in his thirties said.

"What the fuck do you mean, the end?" a guy older than George said. "This isn't the end. This is the beginning. This isn't the end, goddammit."

The two men, who normally got along well enough to play golf together, had to be separated by the others. They were both in tears.

George was surprised, when he went home early, barely after 2, to find Carter there. She had the TV on, like everyone else. She was crying, too.

"They let school out early?" he asked.

She didn't answer at first, then handed him the letter from her doctor, or at least one of his staff.

She was faithful about having the mammograms done regularly. She hated them, called them slam-ograms.

The letter, coolly clinical, said the lump was about three centimeters. George did the math.

"But they can get it, right?"

Carter shrugged and nodded. "Yeah, I'm sure they can, honey. But I've got to go in and get some more tests and maybe, you know, treatment."

She had gotten the letter the day before and had chewed it over in her mind all the time they were watching television, then in bed while George was sleeping. Finally, that morning, with Manhattan burning in the background, she told the principal of the school where she was substitute teaching "so I won't be a total drain on society" that she had to go home. She was the third teacher to do so that day, and the principal assumed her reason was the same as theirs.

She didn't go straight home, instead waiting in her doctor's office for two hours until he had time to tell her that, yes, it probably would involve chemotherapy.

"And maybe radiation, too," as if it were an afterthought. His eyes kept wandering to the TV set behind Carter.

"Goddamndest thing," he said and shook his head. "Godddamndest thing."

After that, it always was easy to remember when they all knew Carter had breast cancer. (They told Jake that day, too, not because they thought he was old enough, but because neither of them could keep that kind of secret.)

Shortly after Carter died, George was looking up an article in the *Times-Dispatch* about one of his company's rivals that had been bought by a large conglomerate. The reel of microfilm was for September 2001. George looked at the paper for September 12.

A woman in Louisa County had died in a wreck when her pickup truck ran off a country road. At Sandbridge, a teenager drowned, pulled out to sea on that heartbreakingly perfect day. A body was found lying in a car in a neighborhood north of Broad Street known for drug deals gone bad. The obituary page had spilled over and taken much of the next page as well.

Misery might not truly love company, George reasoned, but he was pretty sure it didn't want to be completely alone, either.

GEORGE ASKS Freeman where he was on 9/11.

After a pause: "I was on a train. Sudbury to Montreal. I'd been visiting some friends."

"What was it like? I mean, did people cheer, or cry, or what?"

Freeman looks annoyed.

"Fuck, man, nobody was cheering that first day, unless you were living in the Gaza Strip or something. Everybody felt really bad. It was the worst thing we'd ever seen.

"Even from the first, though, even up there in the far reaches of Ontario, everybody knew who did it.

"There was a guy sitting next to me, not even a Muslim. He was a Sikh. He was very pale, and he kept saying, 'Oh, my gott. Oh, my gott,' and we all knew it wasn't just grief. He knew and everybody else on the train knew the wrath of 'Gott' was coming, and who was going to be on the receiving end."

By 2001, Freeman Hawk tells them, he had been living in Canada for thirty years. He had made a life for himself. He'd started out teaching English to the French. Eventually, he was able to teach French to the English. He had lived most of his time in Montreal, going from a twenty-two-year-old worried about freezing that first winter, to renting a bedroom in an apartment owned by a couple who'd left Germany before World War II, to his own place.

He married a French-Canadian woman who divorced him seven years later. He lived with another woman for ten years, "but I never really wanted to have the hearth-and-home thing, no offense."

He'd gone there as a firebrand, the kind of American the Canadian government didn't really want, the kind the RCMP guys loved to make trouble for. He knew that he had to keep a low profile. He helped other draft dodgers and took part in anti-Vietnam rallies, but he was careful to not get arrested.

With his unstylishly short hair and self-contained presence, he was thought, by some in the ex-pat American community, to be some kind of FBI plant.

"I never really had a life plan after I went over," he says. "The way my country waged that war just drained me of anything that you might call ambition, or at least the kind of ambition I'm sure those folks imagined I had in me when they gave me the Williams scholarship. I thought I'd just live my life, work hard, treat people right, fight for truth, justice and the Canadian way, all that.

"Funny thing, though: a lot of those guys who went over grew up to be as much into capitalism as any Republican real-estate guy you ever saw. A lot of them, when Carter gave them amnesty, came back down here. By 2001, there weren't many of us whose belief system bore much resemblance to the one we had in 1971.

"Hell," he shrugs, "maybe they just grew up. Maybe I did, too, God help me."

Freeman Hawk's affinity for the underdog inevitably led him to the Muslim community.

"Kathy and I had this apartment then. I'd always been willing to lend aid and comfort to anybody who really needed it. An easy touch. I had a friend, he was originally from Egypt, and he was working on his engineering degree."

When the friend asked Freeman to come over one night so he could "meet some people," Freeman went.

"Kathy didn't want me to go," he said. "She said Azziz was trouble, that he would get me in trouble. Really, it was Azziz and his friends and everything after that night that caused her to leave."

George gets up to get them both a beer. He has kept up with his old friend sporadically over the years. He realizes, though, that there is so much he doesn't know, and he wonders if he really wants to know everything.

"Go on," Jake says, but Freeman waits until George returns.

The link with Azziz and his companions didn't seem that perilous to him, he says. With Kathy gone, he had the space to let some of them stay with him for little or no rent from time to time, despite the fact that they always seemed to have plenty of money. Freeman Hawk convinced himself that it had to be the well-heeled, the sons of the Arabic upper class, who would change the world. Only they would have the money and intelligence.

He did not really make the connection until late in the afternoon of September 11, although he and everyone else on the train were sure Islamists were behind the attack, even before they pulled into Montreal.

He thought at first that thieves had broken into his apartment. He was at least temporarily living alone then, but the door was unlocked. Nothing seemed to have been disturbed when he peeked inside. He called out for whoever might still be there to come out. He'd picked up a piece of firewood that lay outside the front door.

"Wait, Freeman," he heard Azziz say then, and he and the other two, who had stayed with Freeman until recently, came walking slowly out of the back bedroom.

That's when Freeman Hawk knew he was harboring trouble.

"They have seized the imam," one of the men said as Freeman let himself into his own apartment. "They will make him talk."

"The imam will never talk," Azziz said, angrily.

He turned to Freeman.

"We need a place to hide," he said. "We will not be here long. You need to know, though, my friend. They will be looking at all kinds of records. They probably have been watching us all along."

"What have you done?" Freeman asked him.

Azziz smiled.

"We do not know all that we have done," he said. "We only do what we are told. We are part of something bigger, something that, inshallah, will be the infidels' doom."

He glanced at Freeman when he said this. Freeman had always thought that he was neither an infidel nor anyone's true believer, in Allah or anything else. He was just some-body who wanted to make the world a better place, stand up for the little guy.

He began to suspect that he might have chosen sides without really meaning to, and that the game was on.

"You have been of great help to us," Azziz said, smiling wryly as he laid a hand on his shoulder, "We will be safe here for one or two days, I think, but they will find us, and some day they will find you. And they will know, one way or another, one time or another, everyone who has stayed here in safety."

Freeman Hawk tells George and Jake that he himself did not know everyone who had stayed in his Montreal apart-ment; but he was beginning to see that he could be punished terribly for the acts of people who, in some cases, he only glimpsed, shining eyes and serious beards on faces more committed and hungry than he had ever really understood.

Nothing spectacular happened.

"Azziz and his pals disappeared after a couple of days. I woke up one morning and they were gone. The imam was released from custody."

But there were questions, a slowly tightening noose of information.

"Before it got too tight," Freeman says, looking up, "I got help from a couple of, ah, friends who'd gone from counterculture to drug culture. They fixed me up with a fake U.S. passport. Chris Rainier."

It was almost three years later, in August, Freeman tells them, when he saw a man on the evening news, being led in handcuffs into a police van. Others, the reporter said, were being rounded up. Azziz had a different name, but it was him.

"I knew they'd be coming for me soon," he says. "Azziz was strong enough, but I knew that, to him, I was just one more infidel, an easy prize to hand over so he could protect more valuable ones."

Freeman tells them he packed his few most precious possessions in half an hour and was driving his car toward Vermont fifteen minutes later. Once he crossed, as Chris Rainier, he left the car near the Burlington train station and continued southward.

He had packed his parachute light and well, he says, but he had given little thought to the landing, just that it would take him back into the maw of the beast, the club he had quit thirty-three years before because he didn't agree with its rules.

"I thought," Freeman goes on, "that it was so counterintuitive that it might work. New name, new country. Seemed safer than Belgium or Mexico."

Richmond and George James were not immediately on his mind as he sat on the train headed for New York, but they had exchanged letters. He did know more or less where George lived.

He would not stay forever, he had assured George that day, when he told him his vague tale of harassment from the authorities over anti-war activities, his need to come home. George might not have bought it all, but Freeman Hawk knew that he would be accepted, even if only to help George James make amends.

"So," George says now, licking his lips and fumbling with the coaster that has stuck to the bottom of his beer glass and then fallen to the carpeted floor, "you, ah, you're pretty sure some of these guys who stayed at your place were al-Qaida or something?"

"Or something. Hell, George, I didn't know al-Qaida from Al Kaline before 9/11. They were just a bunch of guys trying to save the world from godless American conquest and consumerism. I was just as appalled as they were about a lot of what was going on down here.

"Then, looking at those poor bastards jumping off those buildings—burn to death or fall ninety stories—with Azziz and the other two, I'd glance over and see their eyes shining, excited, and I knew what a jackass I'd been. John Brown used to be my hero. I guess he still is, because he was fearless and right. But I knew, on 9/11, that I could never be John Brown, or whoever Azziz and his friends were helping along.

"That's always been the dilemma, I guess. You don't change the world by holding little protest marches and staging hunger strikes. You kill the innocent. You give your soul to the cause. Tough trade-off."

Jake is looking out the window, across the park. It's near sunset, and they're getting to the time of year when sunsets at the Warwick are a work of art. Sometimes, George invites friends over on a particularly crisp fall day just to watch the tangerines and reds and mauves change minute by minute on the sky's palette as the just-departed sun colors everything it has left behind.

Today, there are small, golden clouds scudding across the deep blue sky. Below, the park is emptying out. The police will, as always, have to come and remove the last few who believe this could at last be the night they're allowed to frolic after dark, all the signs notwithstanding.

Jake can barely see the man glide along in the near distance, more agile, more fluid than the addled drifters around him. He can barely make out a white car on the street that borders the south side of the park, but he senses that whoever is driving is waiting for someone.

He thinks about remarking on this to his father and Freeman Hawk, but he doesn't. What could he say? "I saw a man who didn't look like he belonged in the park"?

Besides, Freeman knows someone is there.

Jake has heard the stories his whole life, how Freeman Hawk stared down the whole New Hope establishment, how he gave up everything—riches, fame, warm weather—for his beliefs.

Looking at the two of them now, Jake sees that George still believes in Freeman Hawk, maybe more than he believes in God.

Jake isn't so sure. Sometimes, when he doesn't act impressed or even interested in one of George's back-in-the-day stories, his father will look at him, give a half-smile and say, "Well, you had to be there."

But Jake wasn't there, and he wonders if the Freeman Hawk who seemed to be his father's longtime ideal was there, either, or at least the way his father remembers him.

Then was then, he wants to tell George. Now is now. October 3, 2004. We're here. And Freeman Hawk looks a lot better to Jake "then," in some time and place where a father can romanticize him to his son. "Now" is the place where the most powerful nation on Earth would do almost anything to get its hands on a man who had enough of a link to 9/11 to make a very attractive burnt offering. He doesn't have to be guilty of anything much. Jake can figure that out. He just has to be caught. Draft-dodger smirking down on them from the judgmental north, guy who harbored people who probably knew people who crashed those airplanes.

Jake believes in loyalty. It is high on his list of traits to admire. Right now, though, he doesn't know if there's enough loyalty in the world to make keeping—or hiding—Freeman Hawk worth the potential trouble his father seems unable to see.

George stands up.

"Let me get you another beer," he says.

Chapter Eight

The bells of St. Mark's are among Jake's favorite things about the Warwick, even though he hasn't been inside a church since his mother's funeral. Jake always knew that George went along with the Sunday ritual to appease Carter. She might not have been very devout, either, but she insisted that their son at least be "exposed" to religion. Jake always felt, when she said it that way and thought he wasn't listening, that he should wear a lead apron to services.

The slow toll from St. Mark's finally stops at nine. Jake has been lying in bed, half-dreaming, for some minutes, unwilling to look at his watch and see how much of the day he has wasted. He enjoys the floating laziness of being in the sixth-story bed, looking out eye-level at the tops of magnolias.

The church is across the five-sided park. Between peals, a man obviously off his medication screams at passers-by. Jake has long ceased to be bothered by the park's damaged eccentrics. They just seem like background noise, like St. Mark's bells.

Soon, the police will come and take the screamer away, Jake knows. Sometimes, it's George who calls them. He might hurt himself, he tells Jake. The usual procedure calls for the police to wrestle the man to the sidewalk and keep him there, hog-tied with his face scraping the concrete sidewalk, while they take what seems like a casual smoke break.

"Yeah, why should he hurt himself," he said to his father once, "when the cops can come and do it for him?"

Jake is meeting Andrea at noon, at a cybercafé a block beyond the park. They will use the library at the university to work together on their English midterm papers.

He has kept Chris Rainier's secret so far, but yesterday's information weighs on him. He yearns to tell Andrea about his father's mystery friend. She senses, from the couple of times that she's been around him, that Freeman Hawk is not quite as he appears. Now more than ever, though, Jake is determined that no one else will know. He is sure his father hasn't told Carrie. He tells himself he can keep a secret for as long as George can.

Nobody knows, he thinks. Just me and Dad. And maybe, the interior voice comes unbidden, the guy in the park.

Jake gets up in time to shower, then goes into the living room, where Freeman sits alone.

"Where's Dad? And Carrie?" He knows she spent the previous night there.

"Um, well, I think they had to go up and see that lady on the eleventh floor."

"Mrs. Carrington? Is anything wrong with her?"

Freeman Hawk takes a sip of his coffee.

"I think one of her neighbors up there might have, uh, passed away last night."

"Which one?" Jake knows most of the older ladies in the building. Since they've been at the Warwick, two of them have died there, both of them in their late eighties.

"I think George said her name was Hayes or something like that."

"Haigh? Mrs. Haigh?" Jake remembers her for her perpetually, unjustifiably sunny disposition and for the sugar cookies she baked for them last year, leaving them anonymously on the side table outside their front door. It took some detective work to find out who their benefactor was.

"Yeah. Haigh. That's it."

Jake knows she was a friend of Melody Carrington, and he supposes his father and Carrie are up there now consoling her.

"I guess you must have somebody die all the time around here," Freeman says, "with all the old people and all."

The way he says it seems to reduce Mrs. Haigh to an inevitable statistic, and it rubs Jake wrong, the way it would when some fool would say it was "a blessing" that his mother died after her hard illness.

"She was a neat lady," he says, daring Freeman Hawk to dispute that. He looks at Jake, then shakes his head and smiles.

"I'm sure she was. She's probably done the world a hell of a lot more good than I ever will."

George and Carrie return in a few minutes.

"She's fine," he says. "She just wanted somebody to talk to, I guess. She found her. When Mrs. Haigh didn't answer her phone twice, she went down with the spare key and let herself in. She said she didn't appear to have suffered. Just died in her sleep."

Carrie, who had met Mrs. Haigh once, is crying softly.

"It isn't a bad way to go," George says, "lying in your own bed at eighty-five years old. We could all do a lot worse."

Jake wants to tell him that he doesn't think there is any good way to go, then he thinks about his leap into the James the day Butter died, and realizes he is hardly one to wax on about the preciousness of life.

He has a bagel with George, Carrie and Freeman before heading out.

"Too nice a day for homework," the now-composed Carrie says to his departing backpack. "I bet you never see the inside of a library today." He hears his father laugh, too.

He supposes that everyone expects him to do the least productive thing. He supposes he has earned that assumption. What is slightly disturbing is that his father, while claiming he wants Jake to "amount to something," obviously views his mediocre, self-destructive life with at least temporary amusement.

He should be glad, he knows, that slack is being cut. Somehow, though, it bothers him.

He is only panhandled once as he cuts across the park on one of its many paved roadways. At some inexplicable time in the past, it was decided that the park needed several carworthy surfaces going across it, so that now at least an acre of it is asphalt.

"What the hell," Melody Carrington asked once when he was up there on some errand and she looked down at the latticework of pavement, "were they thinking?"

He sees no sign of the man.

Andrea already is seated in the café when he walks in. The crowd is mostly college kids, although Jake does recognize one boy from his American history class.

"I was afraid you'd stood me up," she says, giving him a light kiss on the lips and a mocking smile. "I was getting ready to put the moves on one of these hot college guys."

He tells her about Mrs. Haigh.

"Oh, man. I'm sorry. I'm such a wiseass. I'm talking and I can't shut up."

"I didn't even know her that well," Jake says. The way she squeezes his arm tells him that she thinks every death that brushes him brings the loss of his mother back. Not really, he thinks, but he is shameless enough to accept unearned sympathy.

Jake orders coffee and sips it while he watches Andrea polish off a breakfast burrito with hash browns and orange juice. It never ceases to amaze him how much she can eat without seeming to gain a pound. Unlike him, she isn't really an athlete.

"I just burn it off breathing," she said when he mentioned it once. "Mom says it'll catch up with me one day, but she's like forty-two and she eats the same stuff I do."

They talk about the midterm paper and about going to the library, which is only two blocks away. But they've killed more than an hour, and Jake is on his third cup of coffee, when Andrea says, "You know what? Screw the library. NFW. Let's go to the island."

When she tells Jake she's already halfway through her paper and can help him with his later, he needs no further encouragement.

They walk through the neighborhood between the park and the river, an historically working-class grid that is becoming a haven for professors and students looking for cheap housing within walking distance of the university. Tattooed men and their German shepherds and pit bulls stroll down the nearly empty streets as the sounds of televised pro football leak out through open windows. The men nod and say hello to Jake and Andrea. Now and then, one of them will stop to speak politely and patiently to older neighbors enjoying the early-fall warmth on open front porches.

"My dad used to call this a white ghetto," Andrea whispers to Jake, who advises her to keep this information to herself.

The river is high from recent rain in the mountains. The few brave kayakers below the pedestrian bridge seem to be battling for their survival as they navigate the gauntlet of rocks. Jake thinks he can identify the spot where he once saw the evening star while falling backwards into his family's namesake river, but he isn't sure, and he keeps it to himself.

They begin talking about the imminent sale of Old Dominion Country Hams and his father's continuing claims that he can hardly wait for "the blessed day" to arrive.

"You think he protesteth too much?" Andrea asks.

"Huh? Nah. I mean, he's gotta be a little sad, somewhere deep down inside, I guess. But he knows I'm sure as hell not going to ever want to take it over. And he seems like it's just this thing hanging around his neck."

"Albatross?"

"Yeah. Whatever."

Andrea laughs. "With your fathomless knowledge of English literature, it's a good thing you've got me to help you write that paper."

"Oh, yeah. Albatross. Shit, I knew that. I just don't think about dead sea birds all the time like you do.

"But, anyhow," he goes on, "I do think it's got to make him feel a little, you know, at loose ends. I mean that's what he does. He goes to work."

"Good thing he'll have forty-'leven million dollars to help him get over it."

"Oh, I see," he says, reaching over and tickling her arm, making her squeal. "You're just interested in me for my money. You don't care for my giant intellect and blinding good looks at all. It's all about the Benjamins."

She runs ahead of him.

"Yeah. I'm just going to bleed you dry and leave you for some handsome gigolo. You'll never know what hit you."

He finds it thrilling that they are talking even in jest about something so permanent. When he reaches over and takes her left hand in his right one, she looks up at him as if he's just presumed some intimacy exceeding anything they've done so far in parked cars and quiet rooms. But then she smiles and squeezes back.

On the island, they wander up a path that leads them to such elevation as the island has. Reddish sumac surrounds them, and the trees await the first frost with limp, gray-green resignation.

There are many side paths, and it only takes them three tries to find a semi-private area that is not already occupied. A month ago, the insects and heat would've made this an untenable idea in the middle of the day. Today, it seems perfect.

Andrea produces a joint, and they spend the next forty-five minutes slowly sharing it and each other. Jake uses all his willpower not to push too hard. He wants, almost as much as he wants all of Andrea, not to appear needy.

Andrea, for all her exuberance and seeming lack of inhibitions, reminds him of a stray dog he once spent an entire day coaxing within petting distance when he was nine years old. The dog would come close, tempting him to reach out, but every time he tried to touch the animal, it would quickly jump back. Gradually, the distance closed, and his parents came home to find him brushing the stray, which lay placidly at his feet. All the dog wanted, Jake learned that day, was to feel that he would not somehow suffer for giving up a tiny bit of his raggedy freedom.

Andrea gives to him on many levels, but he knows an attempt on his part to take would spoil everything.

He knows very little about why she's at Barton, where almost everyone seems to have a story, a history. Sometimes, kids seem to try to outdo each other, seeking to establish their street creds.

But when he asked Andrea, a couple of weeks ago, why she was there, she just gave him a little, twisted smile.

"When you know me better," she said, and he left it at that.

They go as far as they've gone so far, despite being interrupted twice by others seeking the perfect space on an early October Sunday afternoon.

They both fall asleep with their backpacks for pillows. Jake awakens first and has to shake Andrea to rouse her. He looks at his watch and is amazed to see that it's 4:45.

She looks startled at first, again reminding him of some feral animal, caught off-guard, trapped and dangerous. It only takes her a few seconds, though, to recover her equilibrium.

"Wow," she says, brushing the leaves off her clothes as she rubs the sleep out of her eyes. "I've never slept with a boy before. I mean, you know, really slept."

Jake doesn't want to know what else she's done. He does not deceive himself that she is a virgin. His main concern is that he himself is one.

They pick leaves and twigs off each other, then slip back down the hill. They are on the east side, and already a late-afternoon breeze chills them.

They emerge into the clearing at the bottom and are in the sunlight again. The island is quickly emptying. Hispanic families cart away prodigious mountains of grills and coolers and folding chairs. College kids, dressed for noon instead of 5 o'clock, walk hurriedly in their shorts and sleeveless tops. Jake is about to reach over and brush a last leaf out of Andrea's hair, which glows now in the light, when she stops.

"Oh, shit."

"What?" Then he sees them. Pete Fallon and three other boys, all members of the Barton team, are in the clearing, not fifty yards from them, throwing a football around. Jake steers Andrea onto a path that runs alongside the river, away from the bridge and away from his nemesis and his friends as well.

They are a hundred yards ahead of the group when they hear Fallon yell out to him.

"Hey! Hey, running boy! Hey, running boy!"

"Just keep going," Andrea says, but Jake knows the path. It circles the island. There isn't another bridge to the mainland for half a mile, and that one leads to the south side. The only other way, he realizes, is to go up, back into the woods they just left.

At a place where the underbrush overlaps the trail, there is a rough path, really just the result of a few dozen people using that route to the top of the hill. Jake pulls her in. They have to run bent over for a few steps, and then they are in the woods. They can hear the boys behind them, and Jake hopes they will run past. He hopes the steady roar of the river's rapids will mask the noise they make as they creep up the hill, farther into the trees.

But when he stops, he can hear them talking, not far below them. He supposes that they were close enough behind to know they couldn't have stayed on the main trail.

His heart sinks when he hears one of them exclaim something he can't make out but yet understands. They have found the path, the only one they logically could have taken.

". . . Either that or they jumped in the river," he hears Pete Fallon say, and they all laugh.

As Jake and Andrea go farther from the water, the noise of the rapids abates, and he knows the four boys must be able to hear every step they take. His only, pale hope, he realizes, is to find another trail, going down, and maybe somehow outrun their tormentors back to the bridge, or to any place where at least there are witnesses.

He pushes Andrea in front and whispers for her to run and look for any kind of path leading downward. He tells her to keep going, no matter what.

"That way," he says, pushing her forward as she breaks into a run, "you can call the cops or something."

At some point, with the other boys crashing through the woods behind them, into the chase now like a pack of hounds, she makes a sharp right turn. Jake follows her. He can tell that they are descending again, heading back toward the river.

He is sure they won't make it in time, that at least he and perhaps Andrea too will be caught and dealt with. He hopes it will be just him, because he doesn't want harm to come to Andrea, and because he doesn't want her to see what happens to him.

He is bleeding from catching a couple of the wicked greenbriers face-high. He knows he is in full panic; he can barely see. More than anything, he's just following Andrea by ear.

The noise from the gun almost makes him soil himself. It leaves him half-deaf, and he thinks for a moment that Pete Fallon and his cohorts are armed.

Then he hears one of them, probably Fallon, exclaim. "What the fuck!"

Another shot is fired, as loud as the first and only slightly less startling. Jake realizes that he is lying flat on the ground. He doesn't even remember getting there.

Then he hears more shouts and curses, and then four sets of feet scrambling off in the opposite direction. Through the darkening woods, he can barely see the silhouette of a figure slipping away at a ninety-degree angle, away from both them and their tormentors. The air smells of metal and smoke. Jake looks over and sees that Andrea is lying on the ground, too, and that she is crying.

"I think I wet my pants," she says, sniffling. "What the hell was that?"

Jake doesn't say anything, just helps her up and tells her they'll get her some dry clothes. He gives her his sweater to wear around her waist on the way back.

They emerge from the clearing and see the sun descending into the cloud bank on the horizon. They are alone, although Jake is afraid all the way across the pedestrian bridge that their tormenters will emerge on the other side and trap them there. He tries to estimate the depth of the water beneath them and the distance to it, and he wonders if he soon will be taking his second dive into the James. He doesn't mention that option to Andrea, who is more concerned about changing clothes than about being ambushed.

The boys are gone, though. By the time they get across the bridge and start climbing the hill that eventually will lead them to the Warwick, it is dark.

95

Chapter Nine

What Jake really does not want to do, if he can help it, is tell his father or any other adult that he is being bullied, that he can't take care of himself. George has always been big on self-sufficiency, and on being so charming, so engaging that no one would want to pick on you. Admitting he was being harassed would be an admission of failure, and Jake has had enough of failure already.

Now, Jake has spent three school days giving Pete Fallon and his friends a wide berth. The strange thing is, they seem to be equally uninterested in confronting him. He still doesn't know who spooked his tormentors away. He can only deduce that the football players think it was him, and that they have had to step back and reassess a boy who might be carrying a loaded gun. Either way, no one else seems to know about the incident on the island.

Yesterday, he was called to the assistant principal's office. His backpack and locker were searched, and the man who doubles as basketball coach would only tell him they had received an anonymous tip about a weapon of some sort. Given his record so far, Jake supposes that the assistant principal thought he had reason to take it seriously. He knows he needs help, but from what he has seen of adults' attempts at meting out justice among kids, he decides he's better off on his own.

Jake is glad to have at least a temporary truce, but he's watching his back. George is fond of telling him that nothing good lasts forever.

Today, he finishes second in the three-way cross-country meet, and all the way, even after he crosses the finish line, his head is on a swivel, looking for trouble.

"Damn," he says to Andrea as he walks her to her car, "I'm so tired of this. God, you must think I'm a real wimp. All I can do is run."

They're at her car. She's driving him home from school these days, often coming up "just for a little while" before going to her own house. He starts to get in on the passenger's side when she turns him around, bends his neck down and gives him a kiss that makes a handful of their classmates hanging out farther down the parking lot whistle and cheer.

"You're so sexy when you run yourself down," she whispers, then smiles at him. "Get in."

When she's buckled in on her side, he reaches over and puts his left hand between her jeans legs.

"I'm ugly, too, and I wet the bed."

She gives him a sideways glance and closes her legs, briefly trapping his wandering hand.

"DPYL."

Don't press your luck. She's smiling when she says it. One of the things he loves about her is that she always gets it. He's heard his father say that the thing he and Jake's mother always had going was the ability to pick up on each other's wisecracks and double-entendres. He called it their secret language. He hopes he and Andrea Cross are developing a language of their own.

She comes up with him, waving at John the guard, who waves back and says something Jake can't understand.

George is home. He's reclining in the Eames chair, holding a martini and looking a little dazed. Freeman Hawk sits facing him, drinking a beer.

"Well, we did it," he says. His grin looks forced, the grin of someone who isn't overjoyed at present but knows he's expected to be.

"Did what?" asks Jake, momentarily disappointed that he and Andrea won't be alone. Then he remembers. This was the day. "Oh, yeah. How'd it go?"

"Well," his father says, taking a sip, "we are no longer proprietors of the Old Dominion Ham Company."

Jake knows his father's progression through alcohol, and he's pretty sure George is now on his second martini, a place he usually reaches—if at all—sometime after 8 in the evening. In the last few days, George seems to have taken up alcohol as his primary avocation.

"Here," he says, failing in his first attempt to get out of the chair, then succeeding after putting the martini unsteadily on the table. "This calls for a celebration."

He disappears into the kitchen and finally, after some grunting, Jake hears the pop of a champagne cork. George comes back in with two glasses for Jake and Andrea.

Andrea tries to beg off, but George insists, and the two of them take a couple of sips after the toast to "happiness ever after, won by the sweat of our blessed ancestors."

"They would've wanted it this way," Freeman Hawk says with a small smile.

George chokes on his champagne. It's actually running out his nose.

"Wash . . ." he says, finally catching his breath enough to wheeze out, "Wash James must be spinning like a top somewhere right now. Although he might think he got the last laugh . . ."

He stops himself, then apologizes and is plainly trying to regain the happy middle ground between sobriety and silliness in which he resided only half a martini ago.

By the end of their senior year, the rest of the campus had caught up with Freeman Hawk. Business administration majors were wearing black headbands and giving gleefully angry fisted salutes. Nursing students turned up for boycotts. Young men who would be in law school in two years and young women who would one day want to burn all evidence of their mini-skirted, braless past seemed to become politically aware overnight.

"Ninety-day hippies," Freeman said in private, ignoring the fact that George had been in a fraternity himself three months ago. "I wish they'd stay the course, but they're annuals. They'll wilt when they go home for the summer."

The New Hope campus seemed to be overrun with dreamy-eyed boys hiding weak chins and acne behind long, well-managed hair and beards. The girls' lank hair hung to their waists.

It reached the point, not long before graduation, when Freeman Hawk came to be looked on as something of a throwback, passed by in the heady, marijuana-scented revolution that sometimes seemed intent on doing nothing more substantial than replacing the Four Seasons with the Doors. Freeman Hawk, whose hair was an unruly mess that fell between the old New Hope standard and the Age-of-Aquarius new one, seldom looked in the mirror before he left the apartment.

He never complained when a dreamy-eyed junior straight out of an Anglophile's New Testament wet dream of Jesus became the leader of the Students for a Democratic Society. (The junior would eventually "right" himself, with help from family friends, and make a sizable fortune on Wall Street.) If Freeman ever was in it for anything except justice, he never gave himself away, even to his closest friends.

"If he can get it done," he told Andre McQueen one day when Andre upbraided him for letting "that little fop" steal their revolution, "let him do it. Nobody cares who does it as long as it gets done, right?"

Andre McQueen just shook his head.

Late in May, George came back from the mail slot waving an open envelope.

"Well," he told Freeman Hawk, "they've got me now."

Freeman had received his draft notice a week before but hadn't told anyone yet. The year before, the night they held the draft lottery, George's number had come up ninety-two, well below the safe point. He'd pulled what he considered to be a well-justified consolation drunk with two other fraternity brothers who were also part of the "sub-century club."

"Shit," George said, "I forgot. You were, what, number three?"

"Four."

"So, have you gotten the letter yet?"

"Yeah."

George was silent for a second. The reality that he truly might be drafted into a wartime army was starting to sink in.

"So, what're you going to do?"

Freeman Hawk looked at him. Then, he took out his draft card. He produced a book of matches lying next to the bong, smiled at George James, struck one of the matches and lit the piece of paper. He held it until it seemed the heat must be searing his hand. Then he closed his hand around it. Smoke seeped out from between his fingers. He never flinched.

George had seen some draft cards burned, and he would see some more burned before graduation. Usually, there was a crowd, and the expectation was that burning your draft card might, if nothing else, get you laid that night. Seeing Freeman burn his card with no one watching except one sometime friend seemed like more of a commitment.

He didn't, then or ever, ask George to burn his. George remembers saying something that day about how he probably would do the same thing, after he thought about it a couple of days.

"What're you going to do now?" he asked Freeman. "I mean, they'll come after you, right?"

He thought Freeman might try for conscientious objector. At a Quaker school, it shouldn't have been that hard, except that the school administration had drifted somewhat from its roots. The one chaplain with whom Freeman Hawk had discussed the war told him that, if he truly believed in God, then surely he wouldn't mind dying in combat. Freeman had almost laughed, before he saw that the man was absolutely serious.

George and Freeman were among the eighty percent of new graduates who did not attend the ceremonies that spring. There was no organized boycott. Everyone seemed to decide, alone or in small groups, that it just wasn't worth the effort any more. Young men and women, some of whom were the first in their families to graduate from anything beyond high school, told their parents that they were going to the beach instead, or they just didn't want to have to dress up and go through a meaningless ceremony.

"Meaningless?" Wash James repeated the word. "Meaningless? My goddamn money wasn't meaningless, was it? Tell me it wasn't. I could've bought a place at Nags Head for what those 'meaningless' four years cost."

"You already have a place at Nags Head."

"Well," Wash said, "I could've bought another one."

George assured him that it wasn't the education that was meaningless, just the graduation.

They argued about it, and Wash even got Clara to call later, but George wouldn't budge.

A week before graduation, Wash James found out his son had been drafted. He was told by another man at the club, a lawyer who heard it from someone whose brother worked at the draft board.

"You weren't going to tell me?"

"Yeah," George said, "I was going to tell you, Dad. I was going to tell you when I got home."

"You need to get back up here. We've got to get you into a National Guard unit or something. I'll start asking around. Don't worry. We'll take care of this."

George James wasn't worried. By the time he was expected back home after a week of partying at Myrtle Beach, he would be in Canada.

Freeman told him, the day George got his notice, what he planned to do. He knew a guy from Duke who had "gone over" the year before. He'd been in contact with him. It was still reasonably easy to get into Canada and relatively easy to stay there. You had to ask for asylum. The guy from Duke was living in a "sort of commune" in Montreal. He said it wasn't that hard to get a job up there, especially if you spoke French. Freeman spoke it fluently. He learned languages as easily as he seemed to learn everything else. George was more of a plodder, but Freeman assured him that Canadian French was so slow and easy to follow that he'd pick it up in no time.

"If you don't like the club . . ." Freeman said.

"Quit the club," George finished it.

He and Freeman went to the beach together, in Freeman's secondhand Valiant, packed in with another boy and three girls. The cottage they'd rented had about twenty people staying there in all. The plan was that Freeman would leave three days after they got there, because his contact was going to meet him just north of the Vermont line the next day.

George was to join him five days later, after hitching a ride back to New Hope and then driving his own car north, past Richmond and into his future.

George James had not really thought it out. He could have admitted, even then, that he was caught up in the moment, riding the crest of his newfound idealism, sure that it would all work out, that he would not be damned to live forever in the frozen north.

"Well," Freeman said as he departed the morning of the third day, with the surf pounding just across the parking lot, "I don't know when I'll get to dip my toes in ocean water again, without freezing them off."

He laughed, dry-eyed. It seemed to mean nothing to him. George loved the beach. For the last three days, he had been making a mental accounting of all the things he would miss in Canada—barbecue, beach music, a good tan, sweet ice tea. Mostly they were too shallow to mention, but he knew he'd miss his family, and he tried not to think about Wash and Clara and Tyler, his little sister who had just turned fifteen.

"It's the first exit north of the border," Freeman told him for the fourth time. "There'll be a parking lot to your left as you come into the town. We'll pick you up there."

George told himself he had to do it, that he had to do the right thing, that one day he would look back on this as the best decision he ever made.

But he wasn't sure.

By himself at Myrtle Beach (although the auburn-haired girl with whom he shared a bed in the overcrowded cottage was certainly some consolation), he tried to drink enough to drown his doubts. He'd sworn to Freeman that he would not tell anyone else what the two of them were planning to do (although he couldn't stop himself, once Freeman left, from giving the girl a few broad hints).

Eventually, though, the party was over. George caught a ride back to New Hope and then packed the few possessions he thought he needed for the long, one-way drive north.

Jake resigns himself to hearing the story one more time. George has become especially fond of telling it in the last year, although this is the first time since Freeman Hawk's arrival.

"I screwed up," he says, shrugging and sipping on his martini. "Screwed up" comes out "shrewed up." "I couldn't bear to leave the country without at least telling Tyler. She was my little sister."

He goes on, almost reciting, as if he himself is tired of the story about how his life changed, or didn't.

"I called in the afternoon, when I knew Mom would be at the club and Wash would be at work. I hoped Tyler would be home from school, and she was.

"I told her I was leaving New Hope the next morning. I told her what I was going to do, and made her promise not to tell anybody. Told her I'd call when I got up there. Told her I wouldn't be gone forever, just for a little while.

"She cried, but she promised she wouldn't tell.

"But she did."

And so, in one of the oldest stories Jake knows, the game is fixed. George recounts how, at a place called Derby Line, on the border, Vermont state police approached his car as he sat stopped, waiting to be questioned and then admitted to his new country. They knew who he was, where he was going, everything.

"When I knew they had me and were going to send me back, some kind of deal Wash had worked out, I made a run for it," he says, his eyes closed. "I got as far as this lake, a big-ass lake with an unpronounceable name. Slept there on the ground. God, was it cold, even though it was almost summer. When I woke up in the morning, I was there on the edge of this lake, and you could see Canada.

"But I couldn't go any farther. By the time the troopers found me, I was a mess.

"They put me in jail, in a town called Newport. See, Wash still had the title to my car, and he'd told them it was stolen. By that afternoon, he was there. And he told me I could either come with him or stay there in jail.

"I should've stayed in jail."

Freeman Hawk comes out of his room for the end of the story.

"I should've stayed in jail," George repeats.

"Nah," Freeman says. "What good would that have done?"

Within two weeks, Wash James had gotten his son into a National Guard unit, and George spent a weekend every month and two weeks every summer as a cook at Camp Pickett.

"At least," he says, as he always does, "they taught me a skill I could use."

He moved out of his father's house, for a while, but he surprised everyone by taking a job with the family business within six months.

No one ever asks George James why he didn't try again to get across the border. Even Jake surmises it wouldn't have been that hard, from what he's heard and read.

No one is about to ask him now.

"You did the best you could," Freeman Hawk says. "It was a long time ago."

George only nods, and takes another drink.

Chapter Ten

George has never been the kind of drinker he wanted to be. He always admired the ones who seemingly could knock back bourbons all day long ("Just cover the ice") without any apparent loss of intelligence or dignity. Only beyond midlife, when their livers began to shut down, would any bill come due.

"He can really hold his liquor," was a compliment paid, not before large groups at testimonials, but in the clubhouse locker room or after a big night of high-stakes poker. It meant something.

George thinks perhaps it is genetic, something carried through the generations in the oldest Virginia families, the ones with whom the Jameses had so much in common, at least superficially. Even the women in the old families seemed to have been born with the knack to drink large quantities of alcohol to little or no short-term detriment. Carter had been like that. She was usually the designated driver after a Kentucky Derby party or somebody's daughter's wedding reception at some club way out in Goochland County, even though she always had a few drinks herself.

Even in college, George knew he had limits, even if he felt compelled to exceed them on occasion. He had a few mornings when he would wake up and feel at one with the world until the events of the night before came seeping back into his brain, no matter how hard he tried to keep them out. Inappropriate comments, indecent exposure, urination and vomiting in public places. A couple of times, he passed out—once in a bar and once at another fraternity house. He was told in great detail by his brothers exactly how unintentionally hilarious he had been. It was humiliating. George James was not without charm, and he knew how to act and what to say, but he hid within himself a shyness, a fear of being a public fool. He had to laugh along with his friends when they recounted his latest misdeed, but he barely could hide the pain.

Consequently, the adult George developed strategies. He'd make sure the bartenders at his clubs and Carter at home knew to serve his drinks weak. He switched to vodka and gin, not to disguise the fact that he drank too much but to keep people from knowing he drank so little.

In the past four days, though, George has been something of a mess.

He made such a scene at a local faux-Mexican restaurant on Thursday night (because he thought someone had been given "their" table) that he was reprimanded by a twenty-one-year-old waitress who said "sir" in exactly the same tone she would have used for "asshole." Carrie and Freeman were able to persuade him to leave quietly.

Yesterday, after two gin-and-tonics, he drove over to watch Jake's cross-country meet. As Jake crossed the finish line first, he could hear his father screaming encouragement. He seemed to be waving a flask.

Afterward, George insisted on taking Jake and Andrea to the Commonwealth Club to celebrate. He had two more gin-and-tonics while they had Cokes. When he stumbled walking down the steps to his car, turning his ankle, Jake insisted that he let Andrea drive the several blocks home. "I'm sorry," Jake mouthed almost silently to Andrea as she turned the Lexus into traffic. She reached over and put her right hand over his left one and said nothing.

Today, George, Jake, Carrie and Andrea are having brunch at the Jefferson Hotel, and it is clear to everyone—including several acquaintances they meet as they troll the buffet line—that George James has fallen off the wagon of self-control onto which he climbed so long ago.

"Who gives a shit?" he says to Carrie, as he accepts a fourth glass of champagne. The rust-colored spot on his wrinkled white shirt is evidence of the two Bloody Marys he bolted before they left home. "I don't have to worry about embarrassing the Old Dominion Ham Company anymore. No family to worry 'bout, 'cept my beaming boy here. Isn't this how the idle rich are s'posed to act?"

Carrie tries to shush him, but he waves her away.

Jake gets up to go back to the buffet line and to escape from George. Andrea follows him. They look back at his father and Carrie Bass, who are in an intense conversation that draws furtive glances from those around them.

"Your dad's kind of fucked up," Andrea says.

"Yeah."

"I mean, it's OK," she goes on. "My dad once passed out on the hood of the car after a New Year's Eve party, and Mom was so drunk she didn't realize he hadn't come in with her. Somebody called the cops and told them there was a man lying on a car in our driveway.

"It's just that, you know, I'm not used to *your* dad acting that way."

"Me either."

They pick their way through the endless brunch buffet. By the time they return to the table, George seems to be in control, or at least quiet.

The pay their bill, and George leaves a thirty percent tip.

"Big spender," he says, winking at Carrie, who does not seem amused.

The cathedral clock strikes one as they return to the Warwick. It is no mean feat getting George into the elevator, or getting him out again. Freeman, who told them he wanted to stay home and read the *New York Times*, comes out to help.

Inside the apartment, they half-carry, half-drag George into the master suite and leave him there on the king-sized bed, snoring away.

"God," Carrie says, "he can really saw some logs, can't he? I mean, he always sleeps on his stomach when he's, you know . . ."

"Sober," Jake finishes for her.

"Don't worry," she says to him, her brow creased. "He's just getting used to it all. Just blowing off some steam."

Jake nods. He wants to tell her that she needn't worry about him. He might even prefer his father's present state to the near-catatonic one into which he slipped after Carter died. At least, these days, George is sober and even funny most of the time, before he slips over the edge.

Jake and Andrea talked twice about their close call on the island, as mystified as ever about their deliverance.

Then, on Friday, as Jake was walking toward the parking lot and Andrea's car, Pete Fallon slipped up from behind and fell into step with him. There were students all around them (Jake tries not to get caught alone anywhere these days), but the other boy spoke low enough that only Jake could hear him.

"That was pretty fucking funny, running boy," he said in a hoarse whisper. "Pretty fucking funny. Next time, you won't be the only one that's packing, you prick."

Jake considered telling him that it wasn't him firing into the trees on Belle Isle, that it was someone else, he didn't know who. But Pete Fallon was already gone, falling in with two other football players up ahead, only glancing back for half a second before they went laughing and swaggering down the steps toward their own cars. Besides, Jake thought when he had time, maybe it's just as well that Pete Fallon and the Barton football team do suspect I'm armed and dangerous.

But who saved them? A little serendipitous gunfire? Some stranger having fun? People did take weapons to the island sometimes. There was a sense that you could get away with things over there. Usually, there were no police unless someone called them.

In Jake's world, Freeman Hawk is the only person who seems capable of doing something like that. Freeman, though, doesn't seem to own a gun, at least not one Jake could find going through his things the last time Freeman went out for one of his late-night walks. And when Jake asked his father, as carefully as he could, if Freeman had left the apartment last Sunday afternoon, George frowned and said he didn't think so, but he wasn't sure.

"Why?" George asked.

"I just thought I saw somebody that looked like him, over on Belle Isle. Must've been wrong, though."

"Yeah," George said. "Probably."

Now, as they sit in the living room, Freeman seems uneasy. He glances out toward the park every few minutes. He's a few feet away from the window, but when Andrea asks him why he doesn't move closer so he can see better, he says he's fine where he is.

Only after Andrea leaves and Carrie goes back to see if George is awake yet does Freeman admit that he's more than a little spooked.

"It's him," he says to Jake, his voice low. "I know it is. He's been out there for days now. I see him looking right at me. And then he slips behind a tree and I don't see him for a while. And then I see him again."

"But you don't see him when you go for your walks at night?"

Freeman shakes his head.

"Sometimes, I wish I would. But they know I'm here."

Jake knows his father is a little worried about Freeman, when he is sober enough for concern. He should worry more, is Jake's assessment.

"What are they waiting for?" Jake asks now. "Do you think it's possible that you're just, you know, a little para-noid? Maybe they don't have any idea where you are. Why would they?"

Freeman turns to face Jake. The tendons in his neck look as taut as piano wires.

"Yeah," he says, quietly, moving a little too close to Jake. "I'm paranoid, all right. Except, if they really are out to get you, it's not paranoia at all. You know?"

Jake nods and lets it pass.

Freeman turns back to the window.

"They're just waiting. They're biding their time."

In a few minutes, George emerges from the bedroom. His face bears the creases from the bedspread, and he looks very old to Jake.

"The dead has arisen," he says groggily.

"More or less," Carrie adds.

They play a game of Trivial Pursuit, with Carrie and Jake on one team and George and Freeman on the other. Freeman suffers from his long absence from American culture, although the others kid him about what they see as an overload of Canada-centric questions. George is still sobering up, drinking water and a soft drink, waiting until the sun is closer to the horizon before he repeats the now-familiar cycle.

Carrie surprises Jake with the breadth of her knowledge, and he is able to hold his own in sports and current pop culture. They win handily.

"Not enough old stuff in there," George grumbles.

"Yeah," Carrie says, "we need to get you two the geezer edition."

"Well, I think it's safe to say a lot of people's feel for the Zeitgeist kind of drops off after they graduate from college."

"Yeah," Freeman says, stretching and yawning, "my Zeitgeist is pretty much stuck in 1971."

George nods, looking straight ahead.

"That was pretty much a suck-ass year."

"One I won't forget," Freeman says.

George is quiet.

In June of 1971, George James joined the Virginia National Guard. It was the same Guard he had cursed a year before, after Kent State.

He didn't go to basic training until the following spring. By then, he was working full time for Old Dominion, being groomed to succeed his father some day. In early May of 1972, he caught the train north, then took a taxi from Trenton to Fort Dix.

George was older than most of the recruits, many of whom were coming straight out of high school. Most were in the "real" Army, and many of those had been given the choice, by a judge in Baltimore or New York or Philadelphia or Washington, of enlisting or going to prison. Some took jail, and some wound up at Fort Dix.

It was, George would tell people later, the most egalitarian environment he'd ever experienced. Most of the sergeants, lieutenants and captains with whom he had any contact in basic training and in cook school afterward were black. George considered himself to be a new kind of Southerner, enlightened and color-blind, but it struck him hard more than once, that summer at Fort Dix, that he was being bossed by African Americans for the first time in his life.

Many of the drill sergeants were recently back from Vietnam, and some of them seemed to bear the interior and exterior scars of their days in the jungle. George had seen "The D.I." a couple of times on television, with Jack Webb as the inflexible but fair drill sergeant. What he saw at Fort Dix was Jack Webb without a moral compass. If there was a common motto among these men, a tattoo on their souls, he thought it probably was "Nothing to Lose."

Everyone knew the war was winding down. George wondered if that didn't make the drill sergeants and their officers even more irate, more inclined to take it out on what one

of them called "you pussy-assed college boys, out there pro-
testin' Vietnam while my butt was in the middle of it."

"Well," the same drill sergeant had smirked at the six
white Guardsmen to whom he was venting his considerable
spleen, "you might get back there to sip your mint juleps at
the country club eee-ventually, but in the meantime, your ass
is mine."

There was very little the sergeants and others could do
that could seriously affect the reservists' futures. Two boys
died of heat exhaustion that summer, in an atypically brutal
New Jersey heat wave, but both of them were Regular Army. A
Guardsman fell off a foot-wide log twenty feet to the ground
and wrenched his shoulder doing the "confidence" course,
and another was recycled because he had pneumonia; but
life could never be a tenth as cheap at Fort Dix as it had been
for everyone in Vietnam, no matter how much some of the
veterans might wish it so. Even the cursing had some rules
attached to it. Far above the men to whom George James and
his other newly shaved trainees answered, were officers who
knew better than to let some rich man's son get mangled in
the Nothing to Lose machine.

Almost nobody going through basic training by then was
gung-ho. Any vestiges of John Wayne had pretty much been
burned out by 1972. The "troubled" city kids were looking
for a way to survive the experience of war, maybe even do
twenty years. The FANGS ("Fuckin' Army National Guard,"
a black dropout from Baltimore had hissed to George when
he looked puzzled at the unfamiliar epithet) were about
doing the four months as painlessly as possible. Staying out
of trouble and having a college degree meant that, as much
as the drill sergeants and lieutenants and captains might
hate them, they usually wound up being class leaders in
advanced training, marching their sullen and less-blessed
brethren to various classes, looking studiously at their ubiquitous clipboards as if they were deciphering great and
important secrets.

The actual physical part wasn't that hard. George was still in passable shape, although he'd put on ten pounds since graduation. He had a better knowledge of firearms than most of the inner-city kids. He had slept in a tent from time to time, growing up. He had been a Boy Scout.

Through it all, though, George felt he had been measured by some unseen hand, and that he had been found miserably wanting.

Even his father, to whom he had handed his future, seemed to treat him with less respect than when they battled constantly over the war. Wash James knew his son did not believe in any of it—not the war, or the business, or even the country—but that he would never leave.

George returned to Richmond only once during the six-teen weeks of training even though he had plenty of weekend passes, especially after basic training. He took the train down to pick up the car he wasn't allowed to have in basic training. He came in the middle of the day, when he knew his father would be at work and his mother would be at the club. He was sorry that he missed seeing Tyler, but he didn't want anyone to know he was there. He left them a note and said he'd taken the car and had to be back that night.

He wrote twice. He also wrote to Freeman Hawk at the most recent address he had for him in Montreal and got a brief, noncommital response three weeks later.

Once, Jake asked his father if he'd kept in touch with any of the people with whom he had spent his brief time in the military.

George looked surprised that he'd asked such a question.

"No," he said. "Hell, they lived all over the country. And it wasn't like we were in combat together or anything."

George has told his son the story of his military experi-ence more times than Jake has wanted to hear it, and even Carrie, in their shorter acquaintance, knows it well enough that Jake can see her glance surreptitiously at her watch, then clamp her jaw shut hard to stifle a yawn. There is something in George's telling that almost smacks of an apology.

"So," he concludes, easing himself back up on the couch, grimacing as his knees pop, "I spent six years doing more or less what our beloved president did, hanging out at the armory, going to Camp Pickett once a month and drinking and playing cards all weekend. Doing my duty, or as little of it as I could get away with doing."

He looks around, probably expecting someone to say something, but no one does.

Jake can't help but glance toward Freeman, who seems not to have heard anything George has said for the last five minutes. He's looking out the sixth-floor window, his thoughts seemingly hanging out there in midair, sixty feet off the ground.

CHAPTER ELEVEN

As they sit across from each other on the Turkish carpet, Andrea lets out a long line of blue smoke from between her pale lips that form a perfect "O."

"So," she says. "Wanna fuck?"

Jake, his lungs full after a long toke, starts coughing uncontrollably, the smoke coming out in little clouds as Andrea slaps his back. Beside them, the window is open. Jake hopes the smell doesn't waft up to the upper floors, toward the Aunts.

"Easy," she says, laughing. "Easy. Didn't mean to startle you."

He tries to talk twice, then finally gets his voice back.

"Are you . . . Do you mean it?"

George is at the club. Jake knows he could be gone for hours. Freeman is out, too, but his comings and goings are less predictable.

Jake realizes they have been working up to this for a while. He has tried very hard not to push it.

With George addled by alcohol much of the time, Pete Fallon and his posse always just around the corner, and Freeman acting like a bomb waiting to detonate, Andrea has been his refuge, his pleasure. The smell of her red hair and her smooth, sweet neck linger long after she's gone. He loves her voice, full of promise without teasing.

She goes with him on long training runs, doing the first two miles of the six-mile circuit, then joining him for the last two on the way back.

They do schoolwork together, and he credits her for helping him regain some semblance of academic grace.

They have gone as far as what Andrea calls mutual masturbation. Her smell is so arousing that he is loath to wash his hands for hours afterward.

He wants "it" and believes she does, too. But he knows that he can't force the issue. Andrea can wield irony like a cudgel when she wants.

Jake has heard the story from a mutual friend:

One day the year before, as she was standing in the hallway talking with a couple of friends, a senior on the basketball team came up from behind and pressed himself against Andrea.

"Do you like that?" he'd asked, humping forward as two other boys watched, grinning.

Andrea looked thoughtful for a second or two and said, "Hmm. Just like a penis. Only smaller. I'm going to call you Peewee."

The story circulated quickly, and the nickname hounded the boy the rest of the school year.

Jake would never admit to anyone that he's a little frightened, and not just (or even primarily) of getting caught. It's been easy enough to perform when only fingers are involved. What if he fails? Part of him is satisfied with the limits of their sexual life. He wants to be perfect, and what if he can't be perfect in the one area that seems so important? Everything he sees, reads, hears or feels tells him sex is the sun that fuels everything. People talk about love and "waiting" and the shallowness of sex without commitment, but all the signals tell him: fucking is everything. And what if he can't fuck? He finds it difficult to believe this could be the case, considering all the times he's gotten himself off (thinking of Andrea lately), but what if?

"I think I do mean it," Andrea answers Jake, not soft and sexy like the movie girls, but straight up, her voice and eyes without guile or coquettishness. "I think it might be time."

That's all she says. When she starts to take off her blouse, he begins stripping, too. They've seen each other's various parts before, but he realizes he's never seen her totally naked until now. And that she's never seen him. He remembers that he has a rubber in his wallet, which is in his bedroom. It's been in there for six months, and he hopes it hasn't gone bad. Right now, he's hesitant to break the spell by retrieving it.

They lie on the carpet, side by side. Andrea's calling the shots now. Whenever Jake tries to make a move, she stills him with her hands. She explores his body with her eyes and fingers and tongue.

"You look good," she says to him. "You look good enough to eat."

And then she slides farther down, so his view is of the part in her auburn hair, with her back and bottom beyond his reach.

When she takes him in her mouth, he gasps. He is so sensitive there that she has to go slowly, taking it out twice to assure him everything's OK. He feels like a small child, but he also thinks he'll die if she stops.

After what can't be more than five minutes, he tries to hold back, then to pull away, but she holds him tight.

"S-sorry," he says, looking down at her upturned face.

She wipes her mouth with the back of her hand.

"I think that's what you're supposed to do," she says, smiling and stroking him. He's so sensitive now that he wants to ask her to stop, but then he doesn't.

When he finally enters her, he is more relaxed, more sure of himself. He was even confident enough to retrieve the rubber, sure she wouldn't get dressed and leave in the ten seconds he was gone.

It distracts him that she wants to talk while they do it, asking him what feels good, telling him what feels good, teasing him a little. He has only heard mythical tales of the female orgasm and doesn't know if she comes or not, but after he fills the prophylactic, he senses that she's ready to stop for now, and he rolls off her.

She looks up at him, pulling her hair from her face.

"Not a bad leisure-time activity, huh?"

"I love you," he says, almost as much out of gratitude as anything.

"That's what they all say." She gives him a twisted little smile that makes him wonder if she's kidding.

He knows how totally uncool it is to ask, but he can't help himself.

"What do you mean, 'all'?"

She pulls back a few inches and gives him an appraising look.

"Well," she says, "I haven't been sitting around in some tower, like some fucking princess, you know, waiting for Prince Charming. You need to deal with that."

He gulps and nods, then just kisses her. He will suppress the image of Andrea moaning beneath some older boy, saying the same things she said to him. Right now, he wants to convey his love and commitment, although he's already aware that his declaration has not been reciprocated.

"So," he asks her, as they lie side by side, facing each other, "you never told me how you got lucky enough to get into prestigious Barton."

She moves back a few inches again, and her smile fades. He's asked her the question before, and she's told him she doesn't want to talk about it. Today's intimacy, though, has given him a sense of entitlement he didn't have before. Everyone at Barton has a story, and he wants to hear hers.

"You really want to know?"

Jake nods his head, and she sits up.

"OK," she says, "but just this once. I'll only tell this one once."

Jake tells her he's all ears.

"That's what I want," she says, leaning against the couch and crossing her arms over her naked breasts. "All ears. And no mouth."

HER DIVORCED parents sent her to Madison Hall, a private school in the foothills that drew old-money daughters from all over, but mostly from the South. There seemed to be no end to parents who believed a few years in the Virginia horse country would be the perfect bridge from puberty to sorority life at Agnes Scott or Sweet Briar.

She was fourteen when she arrived. She was not unhappy to be on her own, partly because she'd always been told that she would go to Madison (like her mother and older sister), partly because she was not prone to nostalgia or homesickness. By the time her mother and younger brother had gotten back into the Lexus, even before the engine started, she was walking away with her roommate, toward her new life.

She saw them at Thanksgiving and over the long Christmas break, but she was ready to return long before her parents took her back in January.

"I don't think Andrea even has a rearview mirror," her father said when his ex-wife told him about it later. "There's just present and future with her."

Her first year at Madison, Andrea's grades were in the top ten percent, enough to get her into the University of Virginia or maybe Duke if she didn't let up, her mother told her.

The next summer went by quickly. She was an excellent swimmer and had little trouble getting a job as a lifeguard at the club. She smoked a little dope and had what she thought of as an affair with a boy who was a rising senior at St. Christopher's, to whom she lost her virginity.

The trouble started that fall. The first time, in late October, she was alone, sitting on one of the low stone walls that surrounded the campus, smoking a joint and watching the sun set between two groves of turning maples. She enjoyed being alone occasionally, away from the almost total lack of privacy in her dormitory. She recalled later looking down the wall and seeing three other girls, all alone, sitting at perhaps fifty-yard intervals, doing more or less the same thing she was.

And that was the last thing she remembered.

When she opened her eyes, she was amazed to see that it was dark. She looked at her illuminated watch, which read 7:40. She was cold and sore and stiff, and she told herself, for lack of a better explanation, that she must have fallen asleep, so exhausted from being up late studying the night before that she had just nodded off sitting up along the wall.

The next time, in mid-November, it wasn't so private. She and her roommate, Caitlin Westmoreland, had managed to get away from campus. Caitlin was sixteen and had her license, and her father let her take the "old" BMW back to Madison that fall. There was a boys' military school ten miles away. A state park lay almost halfway between the two schools, with a back entrance everyone at Madison and Phipps knew about. A couple of the boys were eighteen and had fake IDs. Three more cars were parked there with Madison decals on the bumpers.

They'd been drinking, smoking and dancing to the music from one of the boys' CD players. The weather was turning cold, and they even had a campfire of sorts, fueled mostly by burn logs. Couples would slip away into the darkness occasionally, to the knowing laughs and cheers of the others.

Andrea was with a boy she'd met before. He was a year older and was at Phipps, like most of the others, because of his father's desire to "straighten him out."

Jake can relate. After his arrest, his father threatened to send him to Phipps.

She let the boy lead her past knowing eyes and smirks into the darkness beyond the fire, where he found a bare piece of ground and threw down the military-issue blanket he'd retrieved from his car.

He pulled her down with him, and they made out briefly before he began exploring her more thoroughly, his hands inside her blouse and jeans. She offered only token resistance. Then, she was lying on her back, the boy breathing heavily on top of her. And then, nothing.

When she came to, there were others standing around her, looking down in curiosity and concern. She realized that someone—the boy, she supposed—had covered her enough to spare her further embarrassment, but she also realized she had soiled her jeans, and she thought lying there buck naked could not have been more humiliating.

Nobody knew what to say. A couple of the girls finally helped her clean up as best she could, then Caitlin drove her back to Madison Hall, asking her first if she wanted to go to a hospital. The nearest one was thirty miles away, and Andrea shook her head.

She slept almost ten hours. When she awoke, she was alone. She found Caitlin's keys and borrowed her car (having learned to drive the summer before from the same boy who deflowered her). She drove up to Skyline Drive. A cold front had come through overnight, and at Big Stony Man, the frost had not yet melted.

It was the memory of Alison Gray that brought Andrea there. She'd been a senior the year before when they found her body half a mile off the Appalachian Trail on a January day. She had frozen to death.

Alison Gray had, it turned out, talked about it before, sitting around the dorm room with friends. The easiest way to do yourself in, she said, was to just go up to the mountains, walk away from the trail, take off your clothes and "wait for it."

"If you're lucky," she said, "they won't find you until spring. By then, the animals will have eaten you, so Mom and Dad don't have to pay for a funeral."

She was always laughing when she said it, and no one thought she'd really do it. Afterward, some thought she'd just gotten fucked up a little more than usual and passed out.

Andrea got out of the car and walked fifteen minutes uphill to where the ridge fell off to the west. She was on the edge of the abyss, shielded from the trail by a pair of large rocks. She fingered the top button on her blouse. She heard the crows taunting her somewhere down below.

She stood like that for a very long time, and then she turned around and walked back to the car.

The next day she called her mother and, in a shaky voice that they hadn't heard since she was three or four years old, asked her to come get her. After a minimum of questions, her mother came.

She finally told her, on the way back to Richmond, what had happened. Her mother said, without thinking, that it was just like that with Rose.

Rose, Andrea's great-aunt whom she'd never met, spent the last thirty years of her life at Western State, hearing voices no one else heard.

"It won't be like that with you," Andrea's mother said quickly. "Medical science has come a long way."

"So," Andrea says now, her back turned to Jake, "they poked and probed, did all kinds of tests, and it turns out that they do have some excellent drugs for people like me. But I Googled it, and all this stuff is like pissing in the wind, it seems to me, although I can't get the doctor or my damn parents to admit it. We all agree, though, that it might be best if little Andrea stayed a little closer to home, in case she craps herself in public again. And a nice school like Barton, where they've got shrinks on call, seemed perfect."

There hadn't been an incident since she came back to Richmond, she told Jake. Only a few kids at Barton knew anything about what happened at Madison, and even they were vague on the details.

"I'm damaged goods, though," she tells Jake. "Anything that happens twice will happen three times. Or a hundred and three. It's nothing anybody did, just genes. Bad luck. BFL.

"So, now you know how I got admitted to prestigious Barton."

He turns her around and sees that her eyes are shining. He wraps his arms around her and they lie down together, saying nothing. He puts his hand up, shielding her from the sunlight now streaming in the big windows. She closes her eyes.

They're lying naked on the floor when they hear the metallic fumbling at the door. They earn a few seconds' grace because Freeman still hasn't gotten the feel of the recalcitrant lock. If it had been George, they would have had even more time. When he's inebriated, he can barely let himself in at all. Jake can almost count on hearing the keys fall to the floor, followed by a curse. Sometimes, he walks down the hall and lets his father stumble in.

As they scramble to put on their top layers of clothes, Jake realizes Andrea is giggling. Her lack of fear is one of the things he loves and envies. He stuffs his undershorts in his pocket and hides the T-shirt he was wearing under the sofa cushions just as Freeman comes walking into the room.

"Well," he says after surveying them, "I think I'll go read a while."

Then he smiles, nods and walks back to his bedroom.

"Oh, shit," Andrea says. Jake looks down and sees her panties lying under the edge of the sofa.

"We've got to be more careful," he mutters as she picks them up and sticks them in her jeans pocket.

"I wouldn't worry. I think your dad and Freeman have bigger things to worry about than what the family heir is doing with his study buddy. Nice rug burn, by the way."

Jake sees that his left arm is raw and red. Andrea is rubbing her bottom, and when he pulls her jeans down slightly from the rear, he can see that she also is worse for the wear.

"Hmm," she says, looking at herself over her shoulder in the mirror over the sofa, "I guess you'd have to call this a shag carpet, then."

Jake laughs and says that next time they'll use his bed.

"I hear they work well," she says, and he is thrilled by the implication that there might be a next time.

She leaves in a few minutes, and Jake goes to his room before Freeman can come out and maybe start an uncomfortable conversation, although that doesn't seem to be Freeman's way.

Jake hears George come in half an hour later, heralded by the usual cursing and fumbling. By the time Jake comes out into the dark two hours later, to get a Coke and see if he can scrounge something up for dinner, he can hear his father snoring through the master bedroom door.

He turns on the hallway light and is headed into the kitchen at the other end when he sees a flash to his right. Freeman is sitting in the Eames chair in the semi-dark, shielding his eyes. Something glows red in his hand.

"Fuck," he says. "Turn off the light, man."

"Sorry," Jake mutters and swaps the hallway light for a dimmer one in the kitchen. He takes a can from the refrigerator, retrieves a breast and a thigh from a container of fried chicken George bought two days ago, and heads back, wondering if he can see well enough to make it to his room in total darkness, balancing a paper plate and a soft-drink can.

But when he comes back out into the hall, Freeman has turned on the study lamp beside his chair. The lamp is dimmed, and the room is still mainly lit by the streetlight below, but Freeman still shields his eyes as if he's looking into the sun.

"Sorry, Jake," he says. "I need to wear shades when I smoke this shit."

It isn't like Freeman Hawk to be out of control, but he seems to be tonight. The man who wasn't fazed by stumbling across two post-coital teenagers in the living room three hours ago is fidgeting now. He is rocking back and forth, tapping the chair arm to some unheard rhythm.

"Come here," he says. Jake considers going back to his room, then sets dinner down and walks over.

His eyes have adjusted enough that he can see Freeman's face now. It looks red and puffy, and his shaved head glistens despite that fact that it doesn't feel hot at all to Jake.

"Look out there," he says, pointing out the window to the park below. "Over by that magnolia tree there. Do you see?"

Jake can't see anything except the outline of the big tree across from them. The tree is large for a magnolia. Its top is just above eye level from the sixth-floor.

Then, as his eyes adjust, he can make out more detail—lampposts, the sidewalks that crisscross the park, a couple walking in the distance.

As he turns to ask Freeman what exactly he's supposed to be looking for, he thinks he sees something, a tiny glow from somewhere near the tree. But when he turns and looks at it dead-on, it seems to disappear.

"Did you see it?" Freeman asks. He is leaning forward, next to where Jake's standing.

"I don't know. Was it a light or something? What is it?"

"It's him," Freeman says, leaning back in the chair, looking satisfied that someone else has seen what he's seen, but perhaps also afraid that second-party confirmation has removed all doubt.

"Him who? I'm not even sure what I saw. Just maybe a little point of light."

Freeman shakes his head.

"They sit there, smoking those damn cigarettes. There's two of them. They don't even smoke the same brand. I find the butts sometimes the next day. I've got to get out of here."

When Jake asks him again who or what he's talking about, Freeman tells him that the less he knows, the better.

"Don't worry," he says, patting Jake's hand—Jake can't remember Freeman Hawk ever actually making physical contact with anyone in their apartment before. "I'm going to get the hell out. Shouldn't have come here in the first place."

"Freeman—"

But he rises to his feet, almost falling back into the Eames chair before he rights himself, and staggers off to his room, giving no more answers.

Jake looks out the window again, but whatever he saw before is gone, and he doesn't know if he even saw it.

As he walks back to his bedroom, balancing the cold chicken and some potato chips in one hand, the soft drink in the other, it occurs to him that there is no good outcome: either someone is stalking Freeman Hawk, or Freeman is seriously unbalanced.

George seems to have gone straight from sleeping it off to packing it in for the night. Jake hopes this isn't another step down the slope his father seems to be descending.

Jake takes the chicken bones back out to the kitchen, puts them in the trash, then deposits the bag into the container outside their kitchen. He hears a door open, then the front door open and close. When he walks back to his room, he sees that Freeman Hawk has gone. His clothes and other possessions are still there, thrown all over a bed that doesn't look as if it's been slept in recently. He follows the smell of marijuana to the front door, which he locks, and wonders where Freeman Hawk has gone. He thinks he should follow him, but he doesn't.

Jake lies in bed, reliving this most unusual day. October 14, he thinks to himself. The day I got laid. He has heard other boys brag about their alleged conquests, and he swears to himself he won't do that, even if he isn't Andrea's first. He knows that he would like to be her last. He knows, too, that he'd be wise to keep her from knowing that.

Next morning, he gets up at 6 and dresses for his morning run. He can be out the door by 6:20, get in five miles, mostly in the dark, shower and be ready for Andrea to pick him up by 8. He remembers, seconds after he rolls out of bed, the night before and wonders if anything will be different.

A cold front has come in, and Jake is uncomfortable for a few minutes in just shorts and a long-sleeved shirt, but then his blood starts pumping and he's enjoying the predawn run through Richmond's streets. The garbage trucks and the occasional bleary-eyed dog-walker are his only companions this time of day.

Running down the bike lane on Grove, with the sky turning a pale, flat blue, he thinks he can hear a corresponding set of running shoes on the sidewalk somewhere behind him. Once in a while, he encounters another runner. If the runner is meeting him, they both wave. If the runner is in front, Jake soon outdistances him, and it's quiet again.

This time, though, the footsteps seem to get progressively louder.

Jake steps up his pace, but whoever is back there seems to be gaining. Jake puts on the kind of kick he usually saves for the end of his run, really wanting to leave the other runner in the dust. Suddenly, he realizes the steps have stopped, and he's alone again.

He slows and looks back. There's no one there. When he turns and jogs back to look down the side street he's just passed, he sees a figure turn the corner one block down, headed back in the direction of the Warwick.

As he turns back to finish his run, he almost steps in front of a city bus that he never saw. He sees the driver, a large black woman, shake her head.

Weak after the adrenaline rush, Jake stops and walks the next two blocks, damning Freeman Hawk's contagious paranoia.

CHAPTER TWELVE

On Saturdays, the farmers market gives itself over to the wide variety of goods and food that have come with the city's ever-growing Hispanic population. Andrea says the mercado will give them a chance to try out their Spanish on someone who really speaks it. Jake had just as soon find somewhere warm and intimate. He tells Andrea that George probably is going to be gone most of the day, and Freeman probably will disappear, too, or be in his room. But Andrea says she wants to do something, and the way she says it makes it obvious that "something" is not sex.

The balance between them has changed somehow. He feels closer than ever, as if the sex act had been some kind of binding covenant, and he felt cheated when, the next day, she refused to come up when she dropped him off after school. She said she had to go buy a birthday present for her mother, and when Jake looked hurt, she grabbed his face and turned it toward her.

"Hey," she said. "Don't get all entitled on me."

Part of the change, though, comes from what she told him. He is bright enough to realize that she has shared her darkest fear with him, and that her sharing that counts for more than anything physical.

With that knowledge, though, comes something else: a watchfulness, a tendency to be solicitous. By the time he'd asked her for the third time in three days if she was "OK," Andrea had told him, on the way to school that morning, that, no, she thought she was about to have a seizure right there on Broad Street, and he'd have to clean up the mess if he survived the wreck.

"I'm not going to break," she'd said. "Stop asking me that."

Still, though, he had to check himself yesterday afternoon, as he gave her a kiss on the forehead before going inside. She saw it, sensed what he was about to say. They looked at each other, silent, and he could see the anguish that she'd kept from him and everyone else, floating up to the surface for all of a second before she smothered it.

Today the sun and raw north wind are working magic on her hair. She's never looked more beautiful to him, but he realizes that he's checking her as much as admiring her. He remembers one time, when his mother was in remission and he'd made himself believe she was going to be whole again. They went to a movie, and George kept asking her if she was too warm, or cold, or wanted popcorn, or to use the bathroom.

"George," she'd told him, before the movie started—told both of them, really—"you're making me a little crazy here. Pretend nothing happened, OK? Pretend we're just going to the movies, period. No baggage."

He appreciates, now, his mother's toughness, and he sees that same thing in Andrea and vows to honor it if he can.

They wander among the dried chiles and the smell of cilantro, speaking enough Spanish to make the short, work-hardened people rival the sun with their smiles and respond with long, fast sentences that Jake and Andrea sometimes can follow and sometimes can't.

They've been there for about forty-five minutes when they notice the crowd gathering on the northwest edge of the market.

As they draw closer, Jake sees that there's some kind of confrontation. He stands on one of the picnic-table benches to see over the heads of the encircling audience.

There are two black guys in jeans and leather jackets standing a few feet from a pair of short Hispanic men in work clothes, probably two of the workers at one of the stalls. The Mexicans are not saying much, letting the other two heap abuse on them, but not backing down, either. Perhaps they can't speak English well enough to respond.

"You fucking Mexicans," one of the black guys is yelling. "You fucking spics! You takin' all our fucking jobs. Goddamn you!"

The other man is having his own rant. He's mostly incoherent and looks as if he is more adept with fists than words and might switch weapons at any moment. The two short Mexicans seem as much stunned as angry.

Jake realizes that he knows one of the black guys, the one they can understand.

Lewis Granby was one of the foremen at his father's company. George always called him his right arm. When Jake would come to George's office, Lewis always dropped in and joked with him.

"I got to be nice to you," he'd always say. "You gonna be my boss someday." And he'd laugh as if he'd just heard the funniest joke in the world. George would chuckle a little.

Lewis had his own little office, barely bigger than a broom closet. Jake remembers the framed cornball cartoon that always hung on one of the paneled walls: a funny-looking white redneck looked out mournfully over letters that read, "I pine for you, and balsam too." He wondered if Lewis's white predecessor had hung the sign and Lewis had never bothered to take it down.

George always thought it made him somehow righteous to have given the foreman's job to a black man, but by then, most of the real work was being done by African Americans. Lewis Granby was the man who was capable of managing them.

He had been an all-state tackle at Armstrong High. He's always been a large man, maybe gone to fat a little in his fifties, but mainly just large, wide-bodied. Supposedly, he once tried on a sports jacket at one of Richmond's better men's stores and ripped the lining out just by lifting his arms.

It stuns Jake to see him so angry. He's always been so calm, so controlled. He'd heard George say that he'd only ever seen Lewis angry once, and that was when a young black line worker had called him a "Tom." According to George, Lewis had scared the worker badly enough, just by the look in his eyes as he approached him, that he turned and ran, never to return.

Lewis moves a step closer to the two Mexicans while the other black man stays in place and continues to curse them. Granby towers a head over the two, and Jake thinks they might, like that long-ago worker, turn and run. Then, one of the Mexicans, who couldn't have been more than five feet tall, pulls something out from his pocket. Lewis looks stunned and stops for a second, then sees it's a knife, not a gun.

"Oh," he laughs, and something in the laugh makes Jake think he's been drinking. "Oh, I thought you was going to shoot me. You just got that little boy's play knife . . ."

Before he can say anything else, the shorter man has made a movement so quick that Jake and Andrea, like most of the crowd, missed it entirely. Then they hear the collective "ooh" and see Lewis Granby looking down at his hand in amusement, then surprise, then consternation. The bright red blood shines in the morning light, and someone screams. Now the two Mexicans do run. By the time Jake looks away from his father's foreman, they've faded into the crowd, which itself melts back into its normal rhythm, the two men swallowed whole by it. No one is offering solace to Lewis Granby except the man who accompanied him. The workers are back at their stalls, studiously avoiding even a glance toward the wounded man. The other shoppers have simply and quickly moved away from him, fearful they'll somehow be drawn into the violence that has come out of nowhere to stain this perfect Saturday morning.

Jake moves toward them, even as Andrea tries to stop him.

"Well, that was fucked up," Lewis Granby says, and Jake sees the blood dripping from the back of his hand. "Little bastard was quick, I'll say that."

And he inexplicably laughs. The wound looks superficial, and Jake wonders if the man will bother to go to the hospital or press charges.

Then, Granby sees Jake, and the laugh ends abruptly.

"Lewis," he says. "Are you OK? You want . . ."

The man holds up his hand, blood dripping from it, and Jake shuts up.

Granby and the other man, who looks vaguely familiar, glare at him.

Jake knows he should let it go, but he can't. He follows the two men as they walk away, apparently not eager to be part of a possible police investigation, even as victims.

"What's wrong, Lewis?" Jake asks, trying to keep up with them.

They turn a corner and leave him standing there, hurt and bewildered.

Finally, the other man turns.

"Ask yo' daddy," the man says, pointing at Jake. "Ask yo' mother-fuckin' daddy."

And they're gone.

Andrea is beside him now and pulls him back toward the mercado, but the morning's been almost as ruined for them as it was for Lewis Granby. He can feel the workers casting quick side glances as they walk by and can pick up some of their talk. He knows he's somehow connected, in their minds, to Lewis.

"We oughta go," he tells Andrea after a few minutes, and she silently agrees.

As he's getting into the car, a block away on Main Street, he sees a familiar figure walking away from them, almost to the next corner. By the time Andrea drives past the intersection, though, the man in the suit has disappeared into some alley or shop.

Back at the Warwick, Jake talks Andrea into coming up. He rifles the refrigerator and finds enough ingredients to make a couple of passable sandwiches, then finds an already open bag of chips in the pantry. Freeman's door is shut, and Jake can hear movement within the room. He curses silently.

As they eat off plastic plates in front of the television, Jake picks up the paper. He's looking for the sports section when something catches his eye. There, on the local front, is his father's picture. It's small, just a little rectangle inside a story, with just his last name under it.

Jake looks at the headline:

Old Dominion Hams sold to conglomerate

And then the smaller headline beneath it:

Operations likely to move south

He reads the story quickly. He hasn't paid much attention to the minutiae of the sale, he realizes. He has only been interested in the final outcome: the end of his unwanted role as the Ham Prince in waiting.

According to the newspaper article, the multinational group that bought his father's company has other companies in the same business, including some in Mexico. There still would be a presence in Richmond, a spokesman said, but there would be some coordination of activities "in order to make the company more efficient and competitive." Many workers in Richmond would be offered jobs at one of the company's other locations.

He supposes that Lewis Granby and others who'd worked for Old Dominion for decades must have already gotten the news, and that it wasn't even as optimistic as the version he was reading in the morning paper.

"Well," he said to Andrea, who was reading over his shoulder, "I guess that explains a lot."

"Yeah."

They sit there for a few minutes, most of their sandwiches untouched.

They hear the door to Freeman Hawk's room open, and he wanders out. Jake is shocked at how wasted he looks. There are dark circles under his eyes, and he jumps slightly when he sees them sitting there. How, Jake wonders, could he not have heard us, but then he sees the ear buds and hears the music faintly leaking from them.

"Oh," Freeman says. "It's you. Sorry." Then he walks into the kitchen.

He comes out a minute later, eating a raw weiner, then taking a long pull from the beer in his other hand.

"Breakfast of champions," he says, giving them both a weak smile.

He glances down at the paper lying on the coffee table, picks up the front page, looks at it for a few seconds, then shakes his head as he sets it back down. He doesn't seem surprised.

"Did you know about this, about the company moving and all?" Jake asks him.

Freeman hesitates, takes another swallow of beer.

"Yeah," he says, finally. "He told me pretty much what was going to happen. Didn't know the name of the company, but, yeah, I knew. He felt bad about it, but what could he do?"

It occurs to Jake that "What could I do?" is what his father always said when he told the story about how he didn't go to Canada with Freeman Hawk. And it seems to Jake that Freeman senses that too, offering a twisted half-smile that forms briefly, then disappears. This is what George James does, the smile seemed to say. What did you expect?

Jake wants to hit him. He doesn't know whether it's because of the smug superiority he senses, or because he's known something all along that George hasn't seen fit to share with his only child.

Later, after Andrea has gone home and Freeman has returned to his room, Jake hears the familiar metallic fumbling that precedes his father's entrance. George James almost falls as the door opens at last, and he's face-to-face with his son.

Jake stares at him, saying nothing, then goes to his own room. Only when George goes into the living room and sees the paper laid open to the page with his picture on it does he understand. He nods his head and goes into the kitchen for ice.

CHAPTER THIRTEEN

It's always tough on Tuesdays. The cross country team goes for the longest run of the week, after which Jake either walks the mile or so back home or catches a ride with someone. On a couple of occasions, Andrea has waited for him, but he can tell she's bored. Hell, actually running cross country is boring. If he didn't have some talent for it, as opposed to his relative haplessness with ball sports, he wouldn't do it. Practice is worse. Watching practice must be excruciating.

Today, though, was tougher than most. By the time he got his book bag from the locker, the last upperclassman with a car had left, and he started walking. He wasn't yet out of the parking lot when he saw a flash of red out of the corner of his eye, and then, before he could really think about it, Pete Fallon's ridiculously large truck was pulling in front of him. It was the kind built for work crews, too wide for city traffic, with two rows of seats. Fallon's father had given it to him, everyone at Barton knew, for his birthday.

Usually, the football team practiced so long that Jake had time to dress and leave after the long run. Today, the coach must have shown them some mercy.

"Hey, it's my favorite running man," Fallon said. Jake saw two other players inside, one in front and one in the back, grinning at him.

"Come on," Fallon said. "Get in. I'll give you a ride." He heard the other two laugh.

"No, thanks. It's not that far."

"What's the matter? You too good to ride with the nasty ol' football players?"

As Fallon said this, he turned off the idling engine.

"Get in," he said, and this time he wasn't smiling, just kind of smirking.

Jake heard the two right-side doors open as Fallon took the key from the ignition.

He didn't really think about running. He just ran.

Behind him, he could hear whoops and laughter.

"The chase is on!" he heard Fallon shout, followed in a couple of seconds by the full-throated roar of the engine.

By the time Jake reached the gate, he could hear Fallon's truck behind him, gaining. He ran through the parking-lot gate and across the street, into one of the alleyways that bisect most of the blocks in the older part of the city. Enough trash cans and junk lined the side of the alleyway to make it impossible for something as large as Pete Fallon's truck to get through without doing serious damage.

Jake heard the truck stop and back up, then roar away, headed for the next street down. Jake had walked that way more than once, though, and he knew that there was another, smaller alleyway, perpendicular to the one he was on now, bisecting the block. He took a right turn and followed it. Ahead, he saw Fallon's truck rush past, headed for where he thought Jake would emerge.

Taking alleyways most of the way, he arrived at the Warwick twenty minutes later than usual, exhausted and feeling like a hunted animal.

Now, as he walks toward the elevator, he wonders how this is all going to end. It seems as if Pete Fallon and his friends are going to make his life a living hell forever, or at least as long as he's with Andrea.

Melody Carrington is sitting in one of the chairs that line the lobby. He says hello to her, not making eye contact.

"You look like you've had a rough day," she says, smiling up at him.

He tells her that he's had better, then wishes on the way up that he hadn't been so brusque.

The living room is dark. Jake walks over to pull the curtains back.

"Leave it shut."

He spins around. Freeman is sitting in the Eames chair, his head slumped below the top of it. He reaches behind and turns on the reading lamp. The bags under his eyes are deep purple in the light, and his eyes themselves are red. Even from where he's standing, Jake can smell his body odor, and the clothes seem to be the same ones—black T-shirt and blue jeans—that he's worn for the past few days.

"Dude," Jake says to him, "you scared the shit out of me. And you might want to check out the shower, see if it's still working."

He's pretty much had it with Freeman Hawk. Freeman is like a dark shadow in their apartment, always there in the background, taking everything and giving nothing. Even George seems to be getting a little tired of his old friend. Because Jake has stopped speaking to his father unless absolutely necessary, the place has been exceedingly quiet of late, only breaking into something resembling conviviality when Andrea or Carrie comes over.

"Sorry," is all Freeman says. Jake gets a Coke from the fridge, then comes back in and turns on the TV.

"I'm going away for a bit," Freeman says after a silence of several minutes.

"Back to Canada?" Jake asks, putting down the Coke.

"Nah. North Carolina. Alto, North Carolina. I have a sudden, burning desire to get back to my roots."

His father used to refer to him, in the old stories, as "Freeman Hawk of Alto, North Carolina," as if Freeman's tiny and obscure hometown made what became of him even more amazing.

Jake asks him, after another silence, how long he plans to be gone.

"Dunno. I just need to get away. Fade into the sunset, you know?" He glances toward the window. "I hear Alto calling my name."

Freeman Hawk's father worked as a long-haul trucker, when he worked at all.

"It was about the only thing old Virgil was in for the long haul," Freeman says, laughing feebly.

His mother died of cancer when Freeman was five, leaving behind six children, including Freeman's four older sisters and a brother who was only two.

Freeman has never forgotten the afternoon he came home from school and Virgil was sitting there with three empty Schlitz cans beside him, staring at the blank TV screen. The older girls were home from school already, and they and Aaron were in the girls' bedroom. He could hear sobs.

"Well," Virgil said, looking at Freeman with about as much tenderness as he could spare, "she's gone." His mother's last "bad turn" had happened so quickly that Virgil never thought to get the kids from school before he flew to the hospital, arriving too late.

Freeman barely remembers the funeral. The only picture he has of his mother is old and frayed, and the woman in the photograph, who was still in her thirties, looks worn out, too.

Aaron, the youngest, had been something of a surprise. Everyone thought Freeman would be their last.

"Virgil said he aimed to keep having children until he 'had him a son,' but three years after me, along came Aaron."

There were whispers about that. Virgil was gone for six months at a time sometimes, and it was obvious to all of Alto's 500 or so residents that he wasn't driving a truck all that time. Some said he was nowhere near in the two months before or after little Aaron must have been conceived.

Sometimes, the Hawk family needed food stamps to get by.

"Old Virgil was something," Freeman says. "He was lean as a rail, mean as a snake. I used to hate to see him come home, because it meant the beatings would start again."

No one in the Hawk family had been to college. In the four generations they'd lived in and around Alto, they seemed to have fallen farther behind. If they had any concept of the American dream, it was a hazy image that became dimmer and more distant by the year, the fading lights of a train they'd somehow missed.

Freeman made good enough grades in school, considering how little time he was afforded to do homework and how little encouragement he got. His older sisters were fond enough of him, but for the most part, there was precious little time for doting in the Hawk household. If anyone in their small world could have been said to have been spoiled, it was Aaron. Freeman, the knee-baby, didn't qualify.

"My oldest sister was already gone, married, by the time I started school," he says now as he stares out the window at the trees just starting to change. "In my family, a girl over twenty who wasn't married was an old maid."

The second oldest, Ella, was Freeman's favorite. She was ten years older, in the eleventh grade, when he started school, just a year after his mother died. Ella was a blonde, unlike her dark-haired sisters, and Freeman thought she was the prettiest girl he'd ever seen.

"Looking back now," he says, "she'd probably look a little plain, maybe a little tired, but she was an angel to me then. I wish I had a picture.

"She'd get me up in the morning and she'd be on the bus from the high school every afternoon when I got on at the elementary school. I realized later she could have taken another bus that went right by our house and gotten home a good twenty minutes earlier, but she didn't want me to be by myself. Plus, she missed out on whatever was going on after school."

Young Freeman Hawk wasn't much of a joiner. He says he never really felt the need to be everybody's friend. "Or maybe anybody's friend," he adds wryly.

His first two grades, he learned survival tactics. He became a fast runner, and when boys wanted to gang up on him at recess because he was wearing some of their older brothers' hand-me-downs or he knew how to read better, they usually couldn't catch him.

It was harder to stay away from his father, though. Virgil, in the times he actually spent in Alto between trips, tended to drink.

"One time," Freeman says, "I was supposed to rake some leaves, so it must have been late fall. I had one pretty good friend, Arthur Lee, who lived in a house trailer next to our place. That day, Arthur Lee wanted me to come play something or other. I guess I figured I'd get back to the leaves later, but I forgot.

"When Virgil found me, he grabbed my wrist and more or less dragged me across the yard, swatting me with his free hand whenever I cried. He took me around back, to the pen where the dogs were kept. He always had these damn dogs, even though he didn't hunt much and was gone for weeks on end, just us kids there. But we knew we'd better keep those damn hounds fed and watered, and there had better be as many there when he came back as when he left. Only he was allowed to lose them."

Virgil Hawk opened the gate with his free hand and pushed his son inside.

"There," he said to him, "that's where you can sleep tonight. You cain't do your damn chores like I tell you, you can sleep with the dogs."

Freeman says the thing that really got him was that his father was grinning, like it was a joke. He didn't even seem to be angry anymore.

"It was cold as hell," Freeman says. "I got into the little metal shed where the dogs slept, to get out of the cold, and I just stayed there, afraid to do anything else. He'd beaten me before, and I knew already that, if you disobeyed him when he punished you, it just got worse.

"It got dark, and I could see him in the kitchen, drinking. The girls would come in to get him something, and one time Ella went toward the back door, but he yelled at her and she went away.

"I must have fallen asleep, because when I woke up, Ella was shaking me and helping me to my feet. It was freezing.

"She told me he had finally passed out in his bedroom. It was OK to go back inside. Virgil tended to do it one day at a time. By the next morning, he'd act as if nothing had happened."

The day Freeman officially became an orphan, he was in the third grade.

His father had been home for a few days and had not, to anyone's knowledge, been sober at any time past noon.

"I had been outside, mowing the yard," Freeman says, taking a sip from his beer. "I'd only done it two or three times. Virgil said nine was old enough for me to start doing man's work, and he started me with mowing. He'd told me I damn well better have it done before he got up, which was usually sometime after 11. It was about 10 when I went inside, all proud of myself for having finished already.

"When I walked in the door, I knew something was wrong. Aaron was outside somewhere, playing I guess, and the only ones inside when I'd gone out at 8 were the old man and Mary Beth. She was the third oldest, in the tenth grade, seven years older than me.

"But then I saw the other car parked out by the road. I recognized it. It belonged to Timmy Dwight, Ella's boyfriend, who she was living with. She'd moved out the year before, as soon as she graduated."

Freeman saw the door cracked to the bedroom Mary Beth and the fourth sister, Connie, shared. At one time, four of them had shared it, two of them sleeping on a mattress on the floor, before the two older girls moved out.

He could hear Ella's voice, over the country music that was playing on the radio. Freeman was, for a moment, happy she'd stopped by. Maybe she'd take him to the store later, buy him a 7up and an ice cream sandwich. But then he heard her voice, harder and more grown-up than he'd ever heard it.

"You son of a bitch," he heard her say. "It stops right here."

He didn't hear what his father said. His memory now is that Virgil asked her to wait a minute, that it wasn't what she thought, but he isn't sure. Then, something seemed to impede his father's words. Freeman remembers Mary Beth crying.

And then the sound, not that loud, really, but very serious, like the last word.

He was in the middle of the living room, afraid to go farther toward the cracked door. Ella came out, the little pistol still in her hand. She looked calm, or resigned. She hugged him with her free arm, and he could see Mary Beth in the bedroom, wearing just a T-shirt, screaming. Ella looked back, more impatient than anything else. Then she looked down at Freeman, gave him a little smile and ran her fingers through his hair.

"I'm sorry," she said. "Sorry for all the mess."

He could hear her in the kitchen, calling the police, telling them two people had been shot. It had just registered with Freeman, still standing there, that he'd heard only one shot, when he heard the other one. As with her father, Ella had put the pistol in her mouth. It had sufficient firepower to leave blood and parts of what he assumed were her brains all over the dinette and the wall behind it.

Freeman was sitting outside, on the front steps, when the sheriff's deputy drove up not five minutes later. Mary Beth had run into the woods. Connie and Aaron had spent the night at their favorite aunt and uncle's.

His uncle came and got him and Mary Beth before they took the bodies away. Mary Beth never spoke all the way to the house where Aaron, not yet in first grade, hadn't been told yet.

"After that," Freeman says, "we weren't really a family. Hell, I guess most people would say we weren't one before, but it felt like one, you know. Always lots of kids around. Even with my mother gone and Virgil away most of the time, it seemed like we were a family. Depends on what you're used to, I suppose."

Freeman and Aaron were farmed out to another aunt and uncle, while the two youngest sisters stayed with the ones who took them in right after it happened.

"We didn't see each other much, mostly at school," Freeman says. "The aunt and uncle I stayed with were from Virgil's side, and the others were from Mom's side, and they didn't really get along that well, didn't go to the same church. They were good to take us all in, but I think they must have felt that they were doing us a big favor just to spare us from the orphanage, and that they didn't owe us much beyond that."

Freeman became, unlike his siblings, a stellar student.

"I don't know why," he says now. "Maybe I had a lot of time on my hands. Maybe I was trying to lose myself in something other than my family."

He got in a lot of fights at school and preferred books to people. He could read before he started first grade and can't even remember how he learned.

Freeman puts down the bottle and stands up, then walks back to his room.

Jake has heard the basic outline of Freeman Hawk's childhood from George in bits and pieces over the years, only vaguely interested in the story of a man he'd never met. Now, he isn't sure even his father has heard the complete, unabridged version.

A couple of minutes later, Freeman returns. At first, Jake doesn't recognize the object in his right hand.

"Here," Freeman says. "I want you to have this."

The knife, when he opens it, is about six inches long, and Jake steps back.

Freeman laughs, closes it and hands it to him.

"Easy," he says. "I just thought you might want a little something to put between you and those assholes."

Jake isn't sure how Freeman knows about Pete Fallon and his friends, but he sees, looking at him, that he does. He can't imagine using a knife on someone, but he thinks back to the little Mexican at the Farmer's Market, how quickly he made himself respected.

"Thanks," he says. "Sure you won't need it?"

"I've got something else," Freeman replies, briefly lifting something short and dark from his pants pocket. "Guys I'm dealing with, it just pisses them off if you cut them."

"So," he continues after a short pause as Jake contemplates the only gun that's ever been in his home, "I'm going back to see my family, what's left of it anyhow. Might be the last time for a while. We should have some great time, remembering all the old stories, don't you think?"

Jake looks up, and Freeman's face is wet as he walks past.

CHAPTER FOURTEEN

It's nearly dark when Andrea pulls up in front of the Warwick. The sun has disappeared behind the cathedral, and the chill hits Jake as he gets out, still wearing his purple T-shirt and running shorts. He went straight from the meet to Andrea's car afterward, not bothering to change. He takes his bag with his school clothes out of the trunk, and the two of them go inside.

George hasn't been around much lately. Jake assumes he's spending more time with Carrie Bass. Sometimes, when he gets up in the morning, his father's bed is undisturbed.

When Jake confronted George about the terms of the sale, telling him about his encounter with Lewis Granby, his father set down his drink and looked up at him. He couldn't have been surprised that Jake knew. Everyone in Richmond who could read knew by then. But still there was something in his eyes that told Jake he hadn't really come up with an answer either one of them could live with.

Finally, as Jake walked away, he heard George say, "It was the best deal I could get. Did you want me to close the damn plant?

"Jake . . ." he began. But then he stopped, just shook his head and looked at his son.

"Have another drink," Jake muttered, not looking back as he slammed his bedroom door.

"Alone again," Andrea says as he reaches around and puts both hands in her rear jeans pockets. She reciprocates, and they stand there in the long hallway, kissing. He leads her toward the living room. At this point, he is not very worried about what George might think. The idea that he is entitled to shock his father and dare him to protest only adds to his excitement.

They spend the next hour and a half making love, and then Andrea sits up suddenly, begins pulling up her jeans and tells him she has to go home, that she'll be late for dinner.

"Tell your mom you're eating with us," he says, but she declines. "I'd love to eat with you," she says, giving him a lewd grin, "but tonight is a command performance. My aunt and uncle are coming, and the princess has been told in no uncertain terms that she'll be there, too."

Less than twenty minutes after he lets Andrea see herself out, the doorbell rings. He assumes it's someone from inside the Warwick. The outside doors can only be opened with a fob. Otherwise, visitors have to be buzzed in.

Jake opens the heavy wooden door slightly. Before he can react, it swings open, hitting his forehead and almost knocking him onto the floor.

He takes two steps backwards and is about to cry for help when he sees the small but substantial-looking pistol one of the two intruders is now pointing at him. He wonders if the Wallers, whose unit faces theirs, just across from the elevator, are home. Then the door shuts and he realizes his options are somewhat limited.

"You should know that you need to shut the fuck up," says the shorter man, the one holding the gun. One of the hallway lights is out, and Jake has trouble seeing the man. He is a couple of inches shorter than Jake but considerably wider. There's something vaguely foreign in his accent, and he realizes that the intruder sounds a little like Freeman Hawk.

Jake doesn't say anything, just nods. The man is wearing a black pullover and jeans. He seems slightly nervous, glancing from side to side as he and the other man back Jake down the hall toward the living room. He's as bald as Freeman, but his head is, like his body, unnaturally wide. When they step into the fuller light of the big room, Jake sees that he is of some vague mixture of races, perhaps black and Filipino, or Chinese, although his skin is almost as pale as Jake's. His brown eyes shine, reflecting the overhead light.

Until now, Jake has not had a good look at the second man. As he turns, he realizes that he recognizes him.

"I know you."

The second man steps forward now, not stopping until his face is inches from Jake's.

"No, you don't," he says quietly.

The man is about six feet tall. He is dressed in a black suit with a white shirt, and his shoes are so shined they look wet. There is some gray in his well-tended hair, and he smells of some vague, androgynous cologne. He smiles slightly, his eyes never leaving Jake's, until the boy looks down.

"You don't know me," he repeats. "You don't know me at all. Do you?"

"No. No sir."

Something about the man, as polite and well-heeled as he appears, makes Jake more uneasy than the thug who now stands to one side, smirking.

"Good," the second man says. "I'm glad we have that straight."

He has the same accent as the other intruder, although he speaks better English.

"You really need better security around that basement door," he says, as if he's reading Jake's mind. "It took Box no time at all to get us inside, did it, Box?"

The other man says nothing, just smiles slightly.

Jake can't stop himself from asking, although he thinks he knows the answer.

"You . . . you guys are FBI, right?"

The man in the suit seems stunned for a minute, then starts laughing quietly. Box shows no emotion at all.

"FBI? Yeah, sure, Jake. It is Jake, right? Yeah, we're FBI. Fucking Bad Individuals. Where did you get that? Is that what he told you? FBI?"

Jake says nothing.

Box goes down the hall, carefully opening doors one at a time, his gun at his side. The other man motions for Jake to sit on the couch, then walks over to the window overlooking the park. He sits on the sill, looking out toward downtown.

"Nice view," he says. "Very nice indeed. Our Mr. Hawk found himself a nice place to hide out."

He moves toward Jake, taking a seat on the Eames chair's footstool, his legs slightly spread.

"You see, we've been observing Mr. Hawk for some time, almost since he got here, really. He wasn't that hard to follow. We've been waiting. But now, it seems Mr. Hawk has gone, departed, taken a powder as they say in the old detective movies."

Jake wishes his father were here, but at the same time he's glad he isn't. George might stumble in drunk and do or say the wrong thing. Neither the man in the suit nor Box seems as if he would be willing to overlook insults.

"We have some business with Mr. Hawk," the man in the suit says. "We've been, as you say, biding our time, giving Mr. Hawk the opportunity to do the right thing.

"It seems, though, that he has done the wrong thing. The wrong thing entirely."

Box comes back into the living room. He shakes his head, then hands his partner a single item, an extremely used copy of *The Sound and the Fury* with dog-eared pages throughout.

"Faulkner," the man in the suit says. "Our Mr. Hawk is a deep one, always has been. He might have been quite special, I guess, if he'd taken a different turn, zigged instead of zagged."

The two men walk away from him and speak together, then the one in the suit returns.

"We need to know something," he says.

Twenty minutes later, they leave.

Jake nearly falls as he gets up finally to lock the door after them. His legs, he realizes, are shaking.

The phone rang once while they were questioning him, and they told him to let it ring. He listened, along with his visitors, as George explained that he was at Carrie's and probably wouldn't be back until late (meaning not at all), and that Jake could order pizza "or whatever" and put it on the VISA card.

He should be hungry now, but he isn't, just weak.

He had no reason to trust them, but he wondered why they would lie about it.

Box was mostly quiet, although at one point he spoke to the other man and seemed to call him "Goldie." It passed briefly through Jake's brain that it was odd for a man with black hair to be named Goldie, but he didn't really think much about it, being occupied with other matters, such as trying to understand the true nature of Freeman Hawk.

It wasn't that difficult, Goldie had explained to him. It was about what it always seemed to be about. It was about money.

What Freeman Hawk had done, he explained, was take a large amount of money that belonged to someone else. That someone else employed Box and Goldie for, among other services, ensuring that such things did not happen.

"He knows we're here," Goldie had said. "We've had a few conversations. The gentleman for whom we're working, he doesn't want much, just his money—and maybe a chance to talk with Mr. Hawk, show him the error of his ways."

He winked at Box, who laughed.

"We've been waiting," Goldie went on. "Waiting for Mr. Hawk to retrieve the money he, ah, borrowed. We have been patient, taking our time, of which we have plenty.

"And then, we find that he has, as you say, 'skipped,' left us looking like idiots. Which is why we are hoping that you might be able to help us."

When he said this, Box walked around into Jake's field of vision. He had a small tool in his hand, with a small, triangular expanse of blade reflecting the lamp light. It looked like the knife they kept in their utility room for opening packages and other tasks needing a sharp blade.

He walked closer until the blade was inches from Jake's face.

Goldie, standing at Jake's side, leaned closer and whispered into his ear, "Where did he go? Where did he go, Jake?"

Jake told them that he didn't know, and Goldie stepped back and acted as if he were thinking, considering that possibility.

"Yes," he said. "That could be. It could be that you don't know where Mr. Hawk has gone. Perhaps he just packed his bags and left with nothing more than a goodbye. That is possible."

Goldie took a step sideways so he was standing directly in front of Jake.

"The problem is, we can't know for sure until we've, um, encouraged you to tell the truth. Such encouragement can be painful, more painful than anything you have ever experienced."

As he said this, Box moved nearer. Jake tried to move back from the blade, but his head was pressed against the back of the chair. Box was holding his hair, making him look straight ahead. The tip of the blade ticked his nose.

"Or," Goldie said, appearing thoughtful, "we could just wait until your drunken dad gets home, and we can do it to him. While you watch."

Jake had never considered himself to be particularly brave or bold. Even the events that had led to his arrest for auto theft were more a case of being unable to say no to a bad idea. Even his leap into the river, his presumptive suicide attempt, was something done on a whim, regretted in midair.

So he told them, convinced that he was saving his father, or perhaps both him and his father, from a terrible fate. He told them most of what he knew, remembering the name of the small town Freeman Hawk came from. Alto. Alto, North Carolina.

"Well," Goldie said, "it shouldn't be too hard to find him in a place like that."

He turned his eyes back to Jake.

"I'm going to check this out, see if there really are any Hawks in Alto, North Carolina," he said. "And then maybe we can take you at your word and forgo any further, um, questioning.

"The other thing, though, is this. It would be unacceptable for Mr. Hawk to know of our coming. We love surprises, you see. If Mr. Hawk is not surprised, we will be back, and you will not know either the time or the place of our coming."

Box allowed himself a small smile.

"So, you mustn't tell anyone we were here, and especially Mr. Hawk. I realize that this is a difficult request. Surely you have developed some empathy for Mr. Hawk and might like to help him. But doing so would not be helping yourself or your father, believe me."

As they walked softly, leisurely back down the hallway, they turned off each light they came to, until the door closed.

Just before they left, Jake heard Goldie's voice, distant but distinct.

"You might wonder why we're pursuing this matter so vigorously. I'm afraid I haven't been totally honest with you, Jake. You see, that money Mr. Hawk took? It was mine."

The door opened and then closed so quietly Jake wasn't sure he heard it.

He sat in total darkness for several minutes before he reached for the lamp switch.

Now, WITH the one light on, he looks out the sixth-floor window to the skyline, staying far enough back that no one below can see him. He wants to talk to someone, but he's afraid to use the phone, or to leave. Someone, he knows, could be watching. Someone always seems to be watching. He wishes he'd had wits enough to ask Box and Goldie if they were the ones on the island that day.

As his heartbeat slows and he replays what has happened, he comes to realize that he still might not know the truth. He thinks of the young, bearded history teacher at Barton who told the class one day while they discussed World War II, specifically the Holocaust and Hiroshima, that truth was something to be tweaked, written and rewritten. Truth, he had said, was the property of the victors. Truth could be changed according to who was winning.

Truth, he had said, was priced daily.

Jake realizes that his hands are shaking, and that he is starving. He makes himself a rough sandwich, finding some cold cuts and cheese and washing it down with a Coke he drinks straight from the plastic bottle.

He thinks about trying to reach Freeman Hawk, but he tells himself that he doesn't have a phone number. He can't remember the names of any of Freeman's siblings, whose names he'd never heard until two days ago. He isn't sure what Freeman's plans were, other than to "see his family." He only remembers the name of the town.

Alto.

And he wonders, as he sits back on the couch where he was so recently interrogated, if he really wants to get involved.

He knows he should call his father, but he doesn't. He realizes that George has somehow ceased to be the rock, the center whose gravity keeps everything from spinning off into the unknown. George, he thinks, would just freak, probably make things worse, maybe even get himself hurt.

Something makes Jake think of an evening maybe three years ago, in a world he barely recognizes now, where George James and Carter Bessette James and their son were whole and happy, cicadas sawing through the summer air, kids squealing in the distance as darkness overtook them.

His parents probably had downed at least two gin-and-tonics each by then, to go with the ones they'd had before dinner. They didn't mind if Jake sat with them there in the dwindling day. More and more, they seemed to treat their only child as a third adult. It seemed to please them that they could talk about grown-up things with him. Part of him wanted to stay back, to still be a child awhile longer, but he was pleased that they seemed to approve of him enough to include him in their after-dinner ritual. Sometimes, they'd even fix him a "baby" g-and-t, with just the tiniest amount of gin. He remembers now how adult it made him feel, and also how its bitter taste seemed to be a metaphor for how the world would be when he was really grown: interesting, exciting, but not very sweet at all.

That night, George just blurted it out:

"Maybe we should tell him. About the other one?"

His mother was silent. After a few heartbeats, George continued.

It wasn't the kind of story that should just have been imparted without some preamble, without some rehearsal beforehand, some agreement by his parents that the time had come for him to know.

George and Carter didn't always plan things, though, and Jake knows now that the mundane truth is that probably they were drunk—quietly and sedately drunk, but drunk nonetheless.

So that was the night Jake found out he was not George and Carter James' first-born.

The boy had been named for George, and he had lived for three days, with terrible and irreversible damage.

"I thought, you know, when they cleaned him up . . ." George had started, then kind of choked up.

"But he was just, he was just . . . broken."

The dark had overtaken them, to Jake's relief. He could hear his mother and knew she was crying and wouldn't have wanted him to see her.

Over the years, Jake had wished, silently and sometimes aloud, for another sibling. He was told that it wasn't possible, and then that they were so pleased with him that they didn't want any more babies, that they were just so thrilled to have one happy, healthy boy.

After he knew about the one who died, he didn't ask any more, and George and Carter never mentioned it again.

The knowledge of the brother he didn't have makes him feel all the more alone, though. He envies schoolmates at Barton who have one or more siblings, even if some of them seem to be on the verge of fratricide.

Now, with George gone even when he's home, he feels the emptiness more than usual.

CHAPTER FIFTEEN

Jake left early for school, before George came home from Carrie's and began his daily routine of getting drunk by mid-afternoon. When he unlocks and opens the door a little after 3, though, his father is there. It seems to Jake that the cologne Goldie wore the day before lingers in the hallway like a threat.

George asks him where Freeman is, as if he's just noticed his absence. Jake tells him that he has gone to North Carolina, to see his family.

George laughs, picking up the half-empty glass and draining it.

"Hard to believe," he says. "I didn't think either Freeman or the Hawks cared if they ever saw each other again. I guess time heals all wounds, or wounds all heels."

He laughs again, then grows serious.

"He had it tough, growing up. He was damn near an orphan. I shouldn't be so callous."

Jake knows, has known since the two men left yesterday, that he should tell his father about Box and Goldie, and he can't explain exactly why he doesn't. Their threats don't seem all that dire now, a day later. Maybe, he thinks, he just wants Freeman Hawk out of their lives.

Today, the two of them make a half-hearted effort at cleaning up the detritus from Freeman's stay and wonder, without speaking, whether he will return. Only a couple of dog-eared paperbacks seem worth saving.

"I'm not sure who he is," George says, shaking his head. Jake is silent.

George has moved some of his clothes to Carrie's apartment. Jake often does his and his father's laundry, hauling the clothes to the basement washer-dryer complex in shopping bags. When he went into his father's closet to retrieve the underwear and socks George left on the floor, he saw that the rack where he hung all his dress shirts and pants was only about two-thirds full, and he could tell, from memory, that several of George's favorite shirts were not there.

George and Jake keep conversation to a minimum. One thing they definitely don't discuss is Old Dominion Hams, although Jake knows they should. He wants to tell his father something to make him feel better, but he can't bring himself to lie and tell George it's OK, he did the right thing. He supposes that his father is being honest when he says that he did it for him, but Jake thinks George did it for George, too. He can't imagine his father having to go out there and scramble for a job, find a new way to make a living, like Louis Granby and the other workers soon will have to. He thinks, sadly and uneasily, that George James seems to be looking for a soft place to lie down.

"What did he say?" Andrea asked him when she saw him Monday morning. "I mean, how did he excuse it?"

Somehow, the word pissed Jake off, and he told her it was his father's company, that he didn't have to "excuse" anything.

"My family built that company," he said, as angry as he'd ever been toward her. "He doesn't have to apologize for selling it if he wants to."

She gave him a look, then shook her head, turned and walked off to class. He tried to apologize at lunch, but she waved him off.

"NBD," she said, gracing him with a smile, and he loved her for not making it a deal, big or otherwise.

Jake has pleased his father on one front: His grades have risen to a level last seen when he was in the eighth grade. Jake doesn't really know why, except that maybe he has gotten into a routine. George, he knows, looks somewhat askance at Andrea sometimes, sees her as another wild, dope-smoking distraction for his addled son. Andrea, though, is big on routine. She has a list, and she doesn't stop until each chore is done. Jake suspects that it is all that keeps her sane some days, the stabilizing drudgery of checking things off the list; but he sometimes needs something to keep him out of the ditch, too, and he's assumed some of her habits. Alone at the apartment, they will complete an hour of homework before "jumping each other," to use Andrea's phrase, as a reward for their diligence.

"If you'd spend a little less time with that girl," George told him two days ago, as Jake headed out to wait for Andrea in the lobby, "you might do even better."

Jake turned, his face flushed.

"Yeah, and if you spent less time with 'that girl,' you might do better, too. And maybe you ought to give your bourbon hand a rest."

He left his father standing there, momentarily speechless.

George says that he and Carrie are meeting some friends for drinks, and when he leaves, he transfers the bourbon and water he's just made for himself into a plastic cup to sustain him for the five-minute drive to Carrie's.

Jake calls Andrea, and she rings the doorbell fifteen minutes later. They are supposed to be working on term papers for world history, and they do make a desultory effort before Jake closes a heavy book on Napoleon with enough force to make Andrea look up.

"I need to tell you something," he says.

She leans back, silent.

"You know, yesterday afternoon, after we, umm, did it?"

"Yeah? After we fucked? What?"

He tells her the story he's been wanting to tell someone for the last twenty-four hours.

"Jesus," Andrea says. "So he's some cheap-ass drug dealer, and he stiffed these guys?"

"I don't know. I'm not sure. I can't tell. I mean, he went to Canada and all, just because he had convictions. George used to talk about him all the time, how he was the only truly honest person he'd ever met."

"Well, maybe people change, you know? For the worse?"

Jake doesn't want to think so, but he hasn't seen much lately to indicate that virtue is anything except a very rare exception to the rule.

"I didn't really like him that much," he says, "but he seemed like a guy who didn't bullshit you."

"Convictions." Andrea says it like a curse word. "I think, Jacob Malachi James, that you wouldn't know bullshit if you stepped in it. You're gullible. I like that in a man."

She smiles, taking the sting out of it.

"And now he's down there," Jake says, "some dipwad town in North Carolina, and I've told them where he is. I don't even know how to get in touch with him if I wanted to."

He doesn't mention the full extent to which Box and Goldie scared him, and how that's a big part of his hesitance to tell Freeman Hawk or anyone else about their conversation.

"Well," she says, as if Jake has a simple problem with a simple solution, "maybe we can find him."

"Here's a couple of Hawks." Andrea is sitting yoga-style on the couch with Jake's laptop balanced on her legs. "William J., and one that just says 'A. Hawk.'"

She seems more eager than Jake to "get to the bottom of this," as if it's some kind of game. Jake isn't sure there is a bottom, or that he wants to go there.

There's a phone number next to each name. Andrea calls the first Hawk in Alto, N.C., on her cell phone. "A. Hawk" turns out to be a woman who doesn't seem to know who Freeman Hawk is, then says, "Wait a minute now. I think that was one of Virgil and Martha's, the one that went off to college. Hold on."

She comes back on the phone in five minutes with a phone number. "I think this is the one," she says. "Aaron. He'd be Freeman Hawk's brother. He lives out Bottoms Bridge Road, by the Purolator plant."

Andrea writes down the number and thanks the woman. She turns to Jake.

"We're closing in, buddy. It's your call."

She hands him the phone, which he takes after a long couple of seconds.

"I don't know," he says, holding the phone as if it might be coated with anthrax. "What do I say?"

"How about, like, 'Run, you asshole. Hide. Go low.'"

He makes the call, unsure even as he punches the last digit what he's going to say.

The phone rings ten times.

"Who the fuck," he asks, hanging up, "doesn't have voice mail?"

"Alto might not be on the cutting edge of high-tech," Andrea says.

They try again an hour later, then an hour after that, ordering a pizza in the meantime. It's 9 o'clock, past the time when George might possibly return home, when Andrea says, "Well, there's only one thing to do. Road trip!"

She loves to throw allusions from movies at him, often at inappropriate times, and he's supposed to know the movie.

"Animal House. But this isn't funny, Andrea. This shit is serious. I mean, you should've seen those guys. And you don't even like Freeman."

"Well, it'll be an adventure," she says, as if that will justify it.

"Why don't we just call the police, or the FBI or something?"

"No, they'd just think we're crazy. Or they'd think we're involved."

"Like we're not?"

She smiles. He can see she's enjoying it.

"Like I said: Road trip!"

He doesn't know why he goes, except that he's done pretty much everything Andrea has suggested since their relationship has turned serious. He has heard the crude term "pussy-whipped," but he believes his motivation is on a higher plane than mere sex.

By 11, they're gone. She's told her mother she'll be staying over to finish her history paper, and that Jake's father says it's OK, but, no, he can't talk right now because he's already asleep. She'll be back home by late tomorrow afternoon. Jake can hear her mother's frantic voice as Andrea turns the phone off.

"Better just shut this baby down," she says, giggling, putting the cell in sleep mode. "I think I'm about to get another incoming or five or ten."

"She's going to blame me," Jake says.

"Nah. She knows who to blame. It'll be cool. We'll be back home by sundown tomorrow, podnuh." She makes shooting motions with her two index fingers.

Jake writes his father a hurried note, telling him that he's at Andrea's and won't be back until Saturday afternoon. He feels fairly sure that his father won't bother to call, and equally sure that Mrs. Cross will be calling the Warwick early and often. Sure enough, even before he finishes the note and packs a few things in his duffel bag, the phone rings. Andrea looks at the incoming number.

"Don't answer it," she says. "Let's go. Hope she doesn't cut off my credit card."

"Here it is. It's just a little white dot on some skinny little road. Looks like it's about, um, two inches off the interstate, not more than, like, three, four inches south of the border."

162

"Inches?" Jake looks over at her.

She gave him the keys when they left the Warwick. He hasn't driven much since they took his license, but she said she wanted to figure out where exactly they were going. They stopped at the 7-Eleven down Belvidere where, against all odds, they had a North Carolina road map.

Now, as they merge onto I-95, headed south, she's reading it with the overhead light on.

"Yeah, inches. I can't read the legend, or whatever the fuck it is that tells you how much an inch is. But it can't be that far. Look."

She tries to show him, spreading the map in front of him and almost causing him to swerve into a tractor-trailer.

"Never mind," Jake says. "Just tell me when we get there."

They drive south, Andrea fiddling with the radio and finally giving up somewhere between Petersburg and Durham after a full circuit of the AM and FM dials yields static, country music and a minister whose screeching is only funny for a few seconds.

They stop at the rest area just across the state line and change drivers. When Jake looks at his watch in the men's room, it's 12:45. He splashes some water in his face and looks in the mirror.

"What the fuck are you doing?" he asks the tired face, drawing a sideways glance from a black man two sinks down who seems to be washing out his underwear.

Andrea is sitting in the car waiting for him. She seems so bright-eyed she might've just slept eight hours.

"Here's the plan," she says, backing out of the space without looking.

"The plan" turns out to be nothing much of substance, consisting mainly of directions to Alto, N.C., where they have an address, and the hope of taking Freeman Hawk back to Richmond with them, "or dropping him off at a bus station, if that's what he wants. Whatever."

"If they haven't gotten him already."

"And," Andrea adds, as if it seals the deal, "we know his brother's place is near the—what was the name of that plant you said?"

"Purolator."

"Yeah. That ought to be easy enough to find."

Jake shakes his head, beyond arguing. An expression of George's comes to him unbidden: In for a dime, in for a dollar.

They find the right exit forty-five minutes later, or rather Andrea does. Jake wakes up as they leave the interstate for the quieter world underneath, where suddenly it is really and emphatically the dead of night.

As they turn left on the skinny state road that goes under the shaking growl of the interstate they just exited, a sign ahead informs them that Alto is twenty-one miles away, with only one other named town in-between.

The miles go so slowly that they're both sure they must have somehow missed Alto. As they go around one twenty-five mile-per-hour curve leading up from a creek bottom, a dog, lying partly on the road in front of them and partly on the shoulder, makes a leisurely exit into the woods.

"Jesus," Andrea says. "Did you see that?"

Jake says nothing. It doesn't seem that unusual, all things considered.

In the next bottom, they pass a closed gas station and a handful of houses with a sign announcing a town that didn't rate a spot on the state map: Basso.

"Somebody," Andrea says, "has a sense of humor."

After they've negotiated three valleys, they at last emerge on a flat stretch of highway, one that even offers white lines and a thin paved strip on the side. They pass an elementary school and then a sign: ALTO 1.

"Hallelujah," Andrea says.

Alto, though, never really reveals itself to be a town. They pass several houses, a Baptist church and a Methodist one, a volunteer fire department and a used-car dealership. There is a crossroads, where the thin road they've been on intersects a U.S. highway. To the left, the sign points to New Hope, another dozen miles away. To the right, there is no sign.

At the intersection, there are three stores. To their amazement, one of them is open.

As Jake walks in, the clerk, a man seemingly of Middle Eastern descent walks cautiously out of the cooler, as if he's been hiding there, gauging the menace factor of incoming customers before revealing himself.

They buy packs of Nabs, sweet buns and soft drinks, and ask the man if he knows where the Puralotor plant is, but he only shrugs his shoulders and tries to replicate the word they're saying. Finally, though, he produces a county map.

"Here it is," Jake says. "Bottoms Bridge Road. It's to the left, toward New Hope."

"New Hope," the clerk says helpfully, pointing. "That way."

The road is about a mile to their left, according to the map. They are slightly flummoxed by the fact that every dirt path has a road sign by it. Finally, though, half a mile beyond the last porch light, going twenty miles an hour on the deserted road, they find it, aided by a large sign pointing to the factory at its other end. Andrea turns left.

"OK," Jake says. "It's 2219. So, that's going to be on the left, because 2102 is over there."

They never do find 2219, but, on their second pass-through, they see the barely visible letters on a mailbox at the end of a long driveway: HAWK.

"Maybe," he says, "we ought to park and walk in from here."

He hasn't been able to convey to Andrea how truly spooked he was by Box and Goldie, but something in his tone makes her understand. She just looks at him and nods. They park at the edge of the drive and close the doors as softly as they can.

The rutted clay road leads them slightly uphill. As his eyes adjust to the half-moon light, Jake can see a double-wide modular home perhaps fifty yards ahead. Two large oaks bracket it, and the hilltop space where it sits looks as if it once was occupied by something more grand, something that didn't come in on wheels. As they slowly approach, crunching the dry clay beneath their feet with every step, Andrea whispers, "Fuck. We might as well have driven up here with the brights on and the horn blowing. At least then we could have made our getaway in a hurry."

Jake can't help but smile slightly. He's feeling a little loopy and out-of-body from lack of sleep.

"What's so damn funny?"

" 'Getaway,' " he says. "Who are we, Bonnie and Clyde?"

She laughs out loud, and a dog somewhere in the near distance barks.

"Like I said. We might as well go get the car."

They press on, though. At the front door, they pause, wondering whether to knock or not. The home's owner apparently thought a doorbell was a needless extravagance.

Jake tries the doorknob. It turns easily. The door isn't even closed all the way.

They look at each other. Andrea shrugs, and Jake pushes it the rest of the way open.

One dim lamp barely illuminates the living room-dining room area. The rest of the dwelling is dark.

Jake stands there, listening. Nothing but the asthmatic laboring of an ancient refrigerator breaks the silence.

Andrea tugs at his sleeve and whispers, "What if he's passed out or something? Or he comes back and finds us?"

"Too late now," Jake says, and turns on the overhead light by the entrance. He hears Andrea give out a small, stifled gasp.

The room revealed to them looks as if it has been picked up and shaken. The cheap couch his been turned on its side, its fabric cut. A big, boxy television lies face-down and apparently broken beyond repair on the floor. The dining room table, actually a card table with folded-up legs, lies mangled against the kitchen cabinets. Magazines, newspapers and the home's few books are strewn from one end to the other. Pieces of glasses and dishes litter the floor.

"Hello?" Jake says again, then sees the back door, partly off its hinges with a couple of holes in it that are almost large enough for him to put his fist through.

"I think," Andrea whispers, "that we ought to get the fuck out of here."

Chapter Sixteen

They sit by a window slashed with the first drops of what promises to be an all-day rain, their bacon, eggs and toast barely touched. The four-lane highway outside is almost deserted as Saturday dawn makes a twenty-watt dent in the darkness. The juke box is playing "Something Got a Hold on Me."

They haven't said ten words since leaving Aaron Hawk's double-wide. A quick, panicky search turned up no bodies, just evidence of a quick, unplanned departure. The journey back to the paved road seemed to take an hour. Every footstep was a deafening crunch. Every rustling of leaves in the rising wind suggested they were not alone.

When they reached the car, Jake took the keys from Andrea's unsteady hand after she dropped them in the gravel once. They both felt as if they were in every slasher film they'd ever watched, just waiting for the monster to tap on the window or rise out of the back seat.

But Andrea's car started on the first try, and Jake drove them, somewhat spastically, onto hard pavement and away from the Hawk mailbox. Andrea, he saw, was crying.

Without saying a word, he turned left at the four-lane highway, driving away from Alto, not willing to make that dark, curvy trip back the way they came.

"Better road this way," Jake said, and Andrea only nodded.

They tried for a couple of hours to sleep in the car in a Kmart parking lot but finally gave up.

Now they sit in the Denny's, along with the hung over and insomniac, ten minutes from Alto, and Jake barely registers that they are on the outskirts of his father's college town.

"What do you think . . . ?" Andrea finally speaks.

"I don't know. Somebody's out there somewhere, hurt."

"Or dead."

"Maybe we should call the police," he says. "We could just make, like, an anonymous call. They must have 911 down here. Give 'em the address."

"What if they find our fingerprints back there? They might arrest us."

They interrupt their *sotto voce* conversation when the waitress comes by to ask if they want more coffee. It seems to Jake that the woman is looking at them as if she expects them to either stiff her for the check or pull a gun. He realizes they've been up for twenty-four hours and must look as bad as he feels.

They pay the bill and retreat to Andrea's car.

"What are we going to do?" she asks, taking the keys back from Jake.

The answer he finally gives her surprises her, but she can't think of any better alternatives.

"We'll call George."

He has Carrie Bass's number. He doesn't even bother calling at the Warwick. It's not yet 8 o'clock, and he's sure they'll both be asleep. He'll probably scare the shit out of them both, calling at this time on a Saturday morning.

Carrie answers, groggily, and he is quick to assure her that he's fine, everyone's fine. He hears her call George's name twice, then say, "It's Jake. Nothing's wrong. Everything's OK."

Then, he hears his father's hoarse, phlegmy voice: "What? What's the matter?"

Jake tries to tell the story as concisely and coherently as possible, but George keeps interrupting, asking why he did this or didn't do that. It's exasperating, but Jake plugs on, and finally it's told.

"OK," George says at last. "OK. Let me think." Jake realizes he doesn't really have the kind of advice that will make everything right. He's just stalling for time.

"OK!" he says it again, with more emphasis. Andrea is leaning close to the cell phone, trying to listen in.

"You've got to call Tim Fairweather."

"Who?"

"He's Freeman's friend. Probably the only one he has in New Hope anymore. Freeman told me they still stay in touch. Have you called the police? No? Maybe just as well . . ." His voice trails off.

"He ought to be in the book," George continues after a few seconds. "He's an English professor. See if you can stay at his place 'til I get down there. Lie low. I'm getting dressed. I'll be down there to get you and the girl by noon. No, don't drive back. Lie low. We'll get her car later, or we can drive both of them back. Or something."

Jake tells him not to worry about all the phone messages he's sure to have back at the Warwick.

"Huh? Never mind. I'm not going back there anyhow. Just going to head south from here. . . . Wait! Give me your cell number."

Andrea calls information, and there is a T. Fairweather listed. At first, it seems no one is at home, but then, after the fifth ring, a man answers.

"What?"

Jake is not sure how to answer that question. He explains, as quickly as he can, that they are from Richmond and are looking for Freeman Hawk, to warn him about some trouble.

"I don't know anyone by that name." The phone goes dead.

Jake calls back.

"I'm George James' son," he says to the answering machine. "From New Hope College. He said you used to know him. We need help . . ."

He hears someone pick up.

"This is a bad time," the voice says. "Where are you?"

Tim Fairweather soon gives Jake directions to his house, which turns out to be a one-story rancher in an oak-lined neighborhood three blocks from the edge of the college.

As they get out of the car, Andrea stops and reaches out with her left hand to steady herself on the hood.

"Are you OK?"

She shakes her head vigorously from side to side.

"Just trying to get rid of the cobwebs," she says.

Jake frowns.

"You brought your medicine, right?"

She looks up at him. She's smiling, but her eyes seem slightly unfocused.

"We're going to be home by night," she says. "One day won't make me lose my shit." Then she mutters something else Jake can't understand.

They're watched as they walk up the cracked concrete walkway to the front door, which opens as they come near.

"Get in," a voice hisses.

Inside, they are immediately in what seems to be a combination living room and dining room.

A large couch covered by what looks like a bedspread dominates the room.

On it sit Freeman Hawk and a man who resembles him, only shorter and with dark, curly hair. Freeman is so focused on the other man, who has what looks like part of a sheet wrapped around his left arm, that he has barely noticed their entrance. A dark blot stains the sheet.

"I'm sorry, Aaron," he keeps saying. "I'm sorry, man."

He looks up, finally acknowledging them.

"Welcome," he says to Jake and Andrea. "Welcome to hell."

They sit on the edge of two straight chairs across the room from the couch, not sure what to say. Tim Fairweather, a tall, thin man with a scraggly goatee and clothes he obviously put on in a hurry, takes a nervous peek out various windows from time to time. A halo of wiry gray hair surrounds the bald dome of his head, refusing to accept the inevitable.

"Jesus," he says. "You didn't tell them about me, did you?"

Freeman Hawk sighs.

"No, Tim, like I told you, I'm pretty sure I didn't. If I had, they'd have come for you before now, before I ever got down here." It's obvious this isn't the first time he's been asked this question. "But these guys, I don't know, they seem to be able to find just about anything they want."

Jake exchanges a furtive glance with Andrea.

Fairweather turns suddenly.

"That car," he says, excitedly. "That damn car with the Virginia plates. What if they see that?"

Another sigh.

"Tim, there are hundreds of cars down here with Virginia license plates. It's a college town, remember? If they find us, it'll be because of that damn rented piece of shit I had to drive over here. But I don't think it'd be a good idea to go outside and move it right now, do you? Besides, these two are going right back home, aren't you?"

Jake and Andrea are silent, then Aaron moans, and Freeman turns his attention back to him.

"Hang on, buddy," he says. "We'll get you some help, soon."

Andrea's cell phone rings. She answers, then hands it to Jake.

"Dad? Where are you? OK. OK. We're at . . ." He looks questioningly at Tim Fairweather, who doesn't seem inclined to answer.

"212 Maplewood," Freeman says. "Let me have the phone."

Freeman Hawk tries to talk his old friend into turning around and going back to Richmond, promising that he will send his son and his son's girlfriend back north as soon as he gets off the phone.

"OK," he says after a short silence. "You come get them, then. But watch your ass. We're a little overwhelmed right now."

He hands the phone back to Andrea.

"He's about halfway down here, says he isn't going to turn back."

"What about my car?" Andrea asks.

"Don't sweat the small stuff," Hawk tells her. "There's enough big stuff. It just wastes energy."

From the look on Andrea's face, Jake can tell that leaving her car in a strange town does not qualify as "small stuff."

"Are you sure you're all right?"

She nods. When he takes her hand, it's cold.

Freeman comes over and squats beside Jake.

"You didn't tell them about Tim, did you?" he asks, so quietly that Fairweather, who's walked into the kitchen to peek through the drawn blinds there, can't hear him.

Jake looks at him, not sure until now that Freeman knows how Goldie and Box found him. He shakes his head.

"No, I didn't. I—I'm sorry. They had a knife . . ."

The man pats his knee. When Jake looks down, he notices, for the first time, the small cartoon canary tattooed on the back of Freeman Hawk's neck, just below the collar.

"Tweetie Bird," he says, unaware that he's said anything until Freeman looks up at him questioningly. After a pause, he says, "Oh, yeah. I'd almost forgot. Simpler times."

He sits back, resting on the floor next to Jake.

"It's OK. I just wish you'd have told me they knew, though. Might have hidden myself a little better." He looks over at Aaron.

"My fault, though. I shouldn't have brought George and you into this. Especially you."

"They said you stole drugs. From them."

173

Freeman looks quickly at Jake, then looks away, shaking his head.

"I guess it's time for everyone to go into full disclosure mode," he says after a short silence.

"The truth is, I'd been helping the so-called cause all along, and sometimes, the best help is not strictly legal."

Freeman Hawk had been a middleman of sorts.

"Some of my old friends who'd drifted from smoking dope to selling had gotten pretty, ah, entrepreneurial. They got pretty high up the crime ladder in Montreal. Some of them still are."

One of them, a skinny hippie named Robert Goldstein, who claimed to be from a rich Manhattan family, got Freeman to help him, just small deliveries at first but then larger ones, trusting Freeman with sometimes tens of thousands of dollars at a time.

"It paid the bills," Freeman says, looking slightly apologetic. "And at first, it was just weed."

The relationship went on for years, then decades. Freeman always had a real job, but he made money on the side, whenever Goldstein needed somebody clean to make a delivery. It amazed Freeman that his old acquaintance didn't seem to get any older, and despite his razor's-edge persona, outlived pretty much everyone Freeman had known from Montreal's drug world of the 1970s.

"I don't think we were really friends," Freeman says, "but he trusted me. He'd call me over to sound out something, something he might not have spoken about to another living soul. Sometimes, people got killed. But he seemed like he was above the law, bragged about who was in his pocket. By the mid-nineties, I'd been doing it so long, it was just part of me.

"And then, one day, my two worlds merged."

In that other world, he'd been helping a Palestinian group for years, seeing the irony of this while he worked for a drug-dealing Jewish expatriate. He was mostly raising money. Most of them, like Azziz, seemed to be mainly interested in making life liveable for the ultimate underdogs. If a few of the men occasionally mentioned violence, Freeman Hawk could understand their frustration.

Tim Fairweather was helping him from south of the border, soliciting and sending money.

"No one knew," he tells Jake and Andrea. "I thought I was pretty good at that part."

That day, in 1996, he was summoned before the putative leader of the cell, a man he'd never seen before. The man, dressed all in white, which accentuated his obesity, and wearing geeky black-framed glasses, seemed as much about posturing as Robert Goldstein was. It occurred to Freeman that the two had much in common. The Palestinian was into building power, too.

He said he knew Freeman worked with "the Zionist Goldstein," and when Freeman tried to explain, he shushed him, told him he didn't really care why he worked with Goldstein, but that the connection could be of some service.

What he wanted Freeman to do was be the go-between. He was to tell Goldstein that he had a source who could sell great quantities of cocaine. Freeman would take the Palestinian group's money and pay Goldstein, never revealing its provenance. Then the Palestinians would sell the drugs on the street level.

"We can make very much money," he told Freeman, grinning and showing him a mouth full of rotted teeth that explained to Freeman why the man almost never smiled. "We can make money giving the infidels exactly what they want—their own destruction.

"And the Jew," he had added. "Maybe we give him something, too."

Freeman knew he was crossing a line. Others were joining the group that he knew at first, harder men who said little and kept their own counsel.

175

"Are you a serious person," the fat man asked him, "or are you playing, like a child?"

If Freeman hadn't had Goldstein's trust already, it couldn't have happened. Even with that, it took some convincing.

Goldstein, who had gotten progressively stranger under the influence of drugs and power, and who felt the necessity to act even weirder than he really was in a world where it was necessary to scare some very scary people, was leery at first of Freeman's silent, unknown partners. But it was easy enough to weave a story about sources back in the States, and the money was always paid up front.

Freeman found himself paying for larger and larger quantities as the Palestinian upped the ante. He was always punctual, always alone, on both ends of the transaction.

"Sometimes," he says, "I'd walk up to Goldstein's place with a few hundred thousand Canadian in a briefcase. Then, afterward, I'd drive down the street with a million street dollars of coke in the trunk of my piece-of-shit Toyota, just me.

"They trusted me, both sides. Trust is a wonderful thing. Or a terrible thing."

Goldstein was making a good profit. The Palestinians were sending large sums of money back, often with the aid of Tim Fairweather's laundering. Everyone seemed happy.

"And then, 9/11 happened."

Freeman Hawk thought he might be through with his Islamic connection. For one thing, everyone went underground. Without the Palestinian buying larger and larger quantities, he thought he might break from Goldstein, too.

"Then, one day, I got this call, from my old buddy Azziz, telling me I wasn't through after all, not quite yet.

"They said they needed to raise money, now more than ever, so there I was."

Goldstein was pleased, as always, to have a steady customer, and he never asked Freeman anymore who he was representing.

For two and a half years, Freeman continued to be the middleman.

"I knew what I was doing, who I was helping, but I convinced myself that I was working for the greater good, especially after Bush invaded Iraq."

Then, one day in August, the Palestinian called him, demanding a private meeting with Goldstein. Usually, Freeman himself didn't see the man anymore. When he did see him, the Palestinian had lost weight, and he seemed glassy-eyed, distracted, and Freeman suspected that he was using a bit of the product himself.

The Palestinian said he wanted to meet "the Zionist Goldstein." Freeman had long since tired of trying to tell the Palestinian that Goldstein cared about as much about his Jewish heritage as he did about crocheting.

"I told him Goldstein probably wouldn't allow it, that he had an electric eye out front, could see anybody coming up as soon as they pulled up on the street, and that he never left the house without bodyguards.

"The Palestinian, he was now calling himself an imam, said he had a way, and that I would help him."

Freeman grimaces.

"And I did, which I guess is why we're all gathered here today."

It was easier than Freeman would have thought. He told Goldstein that his source wanted to meet him, that he wanted to make a much larger order, would be bringing five million dollars in cash. He vouched for the Palestinian.

"Goldie told me that it was on me, that he trusted me, and if I said this guy was OK, he'd see him, but it was on me. I was vouching with my ass."

So the meeting was set up. Freeman would bring the Palestinian in his weathered Toyota.

"But I knew he wanted more than a meeting. He asked all these questions. I even told him on what day there would be just one bodyguard there."

The next Tuesday, Freeman pulled up at the assigned no-parking zone in front of a downtown hotel, and a man opened the passenger door and got in.

"Just drive," the Palestinian said. In an immaculately turned-out suit and with his hair cut short, he was unrecognizable, even if he hadn't shaved his beard.

"You don't think the Jew would let a 'towel-head' into his home, do you?" he asked, looking straight ahead. "Only for this would I shave my beard." He pulled down the sun shield and looked in the mirror, shaking his head. "Oh, well. It will grow back."

When they arrived on the quiet street that was their destination, a street of joggers and children playing, Freeman saw the car, parked half a block from Goldstein's townhouse, with four heads inside.

"By then, it was like that old song: Too late to turn back now."

Goldstein's bodyguard let the two of them in. After that, it happened so quickly that Freeman had to replay it in his mind afterward, to get the facts straight.

The Palestinian didn't wait to be searched, instead shooting the bodyguard dead with the Glock he pulled from his pocket and fired even as he raised his other hand over his head. Within seconds, the four men in the other car had been let inside.

"Goldstein was cursing, 'What the fuck?' this and 'What the fuck?' that, until one of them struck him with the butt end of a pistol and told him to shut the fuck up."

Freeman knew where the safe was. Within ten minutes, they had managed to haul it out the door and into the other car.

"The Palestinian walked up to Goldie, whom they'd tied to a chair and gagged. He held the Glock to Goldie's head and made Goldie wet his pants. Then, there was this 'click,' and you knew he wasn't going to kill him. He told

178

Goldie he wanted him to live, so he could remember the time he pissed in his Jew underpants and cried for his life."

He unzipped his pants then, and urinated all over Goldstein, aiming mostly for his face, as the others laughed.

Then the Palestinian told two of the other men to "secure" Freeman, too.

"You are free now, Freeman," he said, laughing, after they'd subdued him and tied him up. "At least you are free if you can free yourself before this Jew pig frees himself. If the pig gets free first, you are, I think, in for a very long day. In any case, we thank you for your help in this matter. We won't be needing you anymore."

They were gone, and then there was silence, just an occasional groan from the bodyguard, who wasn't quite dead yet, and Goldstein's muffled voice trying to break through the gag as he fought to free his arms and legs.

"I told him that they had set me up, that I didn't know about any of this shit, that I was just the driver, but I could see the look in his eyes. It was all I needed to see. He wasn't buying a goddamn word of it."

Perhaps they wanted to give him a fighting chance, or maybe they were just sloppy tying his hands as they left, but he was able to free himself before Goldstein. He thought about untying the man, "but I knew, absolutely knew, that he held me responsible for everything. It turned out there was more than ten million dollars in that safe. Plus killing the bodyguard. And being pissed on. It was a no-hoper.

"I thought about shooting him, right there, and maybe I should have. The bodyguard's gun was still in his hand. Could've made it look like maybe the bodyguard was involved.

"But I didn't. I've never shot anything in my whole damn life. Been close a couple of times, but I just couldn't do it, not even to Goldstein, even knowing what he'd do to me if he ever caught me.

"So I ran."

Freeman had a friend in a town near the border with whom he stayed for a while, but eventually he knew he had to get farther away. He had the fake ID, and he deduced that the country he'd left was a good place to hide out. He knew the terrain, still had some old friends and acquaintances.

He was afraid that by now Goldstein would have found out about Tim Fairweather, whom he had told the basic details about the unfortunate end to their enterprise.

"I've been peeking out of windows for two damn months," Fairweather says, as he does just that.

"I thought maybe I was home free," Freeman says. "Huh. Maybe not home, but free anyhow. Then I started seeing guys in the park, other places. And one day, I got the binoculars, and I was finally able to ID the one. Box."

Box, he explains to Jake, is a cousin of the bodyguard who was killed.

"I guess Goldie picked him specially for this. Don't know why they didn't move before they did. Picking wings off flies, I suppose."

He turns to Jake.

"Your dad was very kind to take me in, but I don't know if he'd have done it if he knew everything."

He says it without any visible regret.

Jake is thinking it is possible that his father has been a fool.

CHAPTER SEVENTEEN

By noon, the rainy morning has become only marginally brighter. At one point, Fairweather's phone rings.

"Geez. You can't come any sooner? We could use some help here."

He hangs up.

"Son of a bitch," he says. "Son of a bitch."

The doctor, a friend of Fairweather's since graduate school, was at a lodge somewhere west of Asheville, enjoying a long weekend with her kids. She was the only one he felt he could trust to look after a gunshot victim who couldn't be taken to a hospital, but she was having trouble getting away. And she didn't seem at all happy to be rushing back to New Hope, all hope of quality time with her children shot to hell. She said she might be able to leave by mid-afternoon, be there by 8 or so.

"No," Fairweather answers Freeman, "she doesn't have any associates I can trust. Not with this much shit."

"I'm OK," Aaron tells his brother. "I think it's stopped bleeding."

Freeman lifts the makeshift bandage and grimaces. The sheet wrapping the wounded arm is soaked. Jake hears Andrea give a little moan, and he reaches for her hand, which feels colder than before.

"That'll teach you to open your door to black sheep," Freeman says. Aaron smiles back, with what seems like an effort.

Freeman Hawk arrived on his brother's doorstep (consisting of several cinder blocks piled atop each other) on Wednesday. He hadn't seen Aaron in more than twenty years and hadn't written him in three. (He was somewhat amazed that his brother hadn't changed addresses, still had the same phone number.) But Aaron took him in anyway, because he was family.

Aaron didn't ask many questions, and Freeman's answers indicated that it would be wise to keep it that way.

"I didn't think anyone would find us," Freeman says, glancing at Jake. "I thought I'd just hide out a bit, then go somewhere else. Tim was trying to help me out with that."

He laughs.

"I even thought what a hoot it'd be to come back to my old college town, settle down incognito, you know?"

"You might have picked a less-conspicuous nom de plume than Chris Rainier," Fairweather says, his back to them as he checks the window once again.

"Yeah, well. You never know what's going to trip you up. Seemed like a good idea at the time."

Friday night, they went out to a bar, against Freeman's best instincts, then got home around 10 and were watching a movie on TV and drinking beer when they heard Aaron's collie-chow mutt barking and growling. The dog made a strange sound, and then nothing.

Aaron got up to check, but Freeman caught his arm.

"Wait," he said, and he slipped over next to the window facing the driveway.

"Come on," he told his brother, heading toward the back door. "Now!"

His expression made Aaron get up and follow.

The back door faced the woods. Freeman cracked it for a second, then told Aaron to run.

They had only taken a couple of steps when he heard his brother's cry and the gunshot at more or less the same instant. He grabbed him to keep him from falling, and they crashed into the woods, dodging trees and getting tangled in briers, not looking back.

"This way," Aaron said. He was in obvious pain, but he had better night vision and knew where the path was. Freeman figures they were at least a hundred yards into the swampy woods when they came to an opening. It wasn't much—he could still feel the limbs reaching out, grabbing him—but it was enough.

Freeman doesn't know how long they walked before they came to a clay road that led to a paved one, and he saw that it was the one that went by his brother's driveway.

They kept to the ditch, Aaron occasionally moaning. Freeman had ascertained by now that his brother had been shot in the upper arm, and that he was bleeding profusely.

When they reached the drive, Freeman made his brother stay by the road while he crept, staying off the gravel path, to the rental car. Every step of the way, he was expecting to be ambushed, but it never happened. Inside the double-wide, it was quiet. The lights were still on. He waited to see if the two men he'd seen when he peeked through the curtains, the ones he recognized from Montreal and then from Richmond, were waiting there. They could have run off, fearing that the local cops would arrive any minute. Maybe they'd figured Freeman Hawk wasn't in a position to call the police, but they couldn't be sure a neighbor wouldn't.

But then he saw a shadow pass in front of one of the windows, and he knew at least one of them was still inside.

His rental car was parked alongside another one he didn't recognize. He wondered why Box and Goldie hadn't blocked the drive. He unlocked his car and slid as quietly as he could into the driver's seat. He knew it was a more or less straight shot behind him to the road, where Aaron was waiting. He knew he had to do three things well, and more or less all at once.

He had the gun out, the one he bought after he let Robert Goldstein live, sensing he'd need it someday.

As he turned the ignition key with his right hand, then dropped the automatic into reverse, he fired at the other rental car's right-front tire with his left. As the car hurtled backwards, he prayed that he was going in a straight line.

He heard the front door burst open before he'd hit the end of the lane, where he stopped long enough for Aaron to throw himself in the backseat, then screeched off into the night.

"Hang on," he told his brother. "I know a place."

"I thought any second I'd see them in the rearview window, coming up fast," Freeman tells them. "I wasn't sure if I'd hit the tire or not. I just knew we had to get out of there. And we couldn't really call the police."

Jake starts to say something, then looks at Freeman Hawk and knows he doesn't have to say it: it was only Freeman who couldn't afford to call the police. His brother was only guilty of being sucked into something he knew nothing about.

He asks Jake if he and Andrea saw anything unusual at the double-wide.

"Other than that the place looked like it was hit by a tornado? No."

Jake doesn't see much sense in bothering to tell them about the mongrel he saw on the way out, lying dead beneath a tree.

"Damn," Freeman says. "They must think I took some of the money with me."

Jake wonders out loud why the police hadn't come before he got there.

"Somebody had to have heard all that," he says.

"I don't think it's that unusual to hear a little gunfire on a Saturday night in Alto, North Carolina," Freeman says.

Aaron laughs, then winces, nodding his head silently.

They'd awakened Tim Fairweather sometime after midnight, not sure what else to do.

"Maybe they went back north," Jake says.

"I once went with Goldie to this house, years ago," Freeman tells him. "They had a guy inside, tied up. He looked like he'd been beaten about half to death, his eyes swollen shut, teeth missing. Goldie said he'd stolen from him, meaning he'd shorted Goldie somehow on some dope. It wasn't much, I think about five hundred dollars. But Goldie said that wasn't the point.

"I think he just wanted me to see what happened to people who cheated him. He couldn't afford to have that happen.

"We left, but I knew they weren't through with the guy."

"I don't need to hear this shit," Fairweather says from the window.

"If you don't get away from there," Freeman says, "I might shoot you. Jesus, Tim, it'll be easy to find me. I'll be in the house where the old white guy keeps peeking out from behind the curtains."

Fairweather moves away from the window, not sure if Freeman is kidding, then turns and goes back.

"I told you . . ." Freeman starts.

"Car door. Somebody's out there."

Freeman walks over to the window, then sighs and turns back to Jake and Andrea.

"It's George."

He makes his way unsteadily to the front door, looking dazed and hung over. When he stops for a second as if he isn't sure what to do, Fairweather cracks the door and tells him to get the fuck inside.

"Tim?" George says, brightening as if he's run into an old friend at a class reunion. "Tim Fairweather? Damn."

They pull him in. He looks at Aaron, then at his son and Andrea, then at Freeman Hawk.

"Hey, George," Freeman says, not getting up. "How's it going?"

George James stares at his old friend.

"I'm sorry, buddy," Freeman says, "but things just aren't what they appear to be sometimes. Items seen in the rear-view mirror may be weirder than they appear."

Jake has given his father the basic details, and Freeman fills George in on much of the rest as George slowly takes a seat in a beanbag chair. Sliding down into the incongruous contraption, the first one he's seen in more than a decade, he feels as if he's slipped into a time machine, except the past has been changed. He is trying to process what he's just heard, distracted by a throbbing headache and the knowledge that he needs to get Jake and Andrea out of here. He realizes he must look somewhat stunned.

Freeman leans down and puts his hands on George's shoulders.

"Man, it isn't as simple as you think it is," he tells him. "How could you be a goddamn captain of industry and not understand that? Sometimes the devil can help you. And sometimes it's hard to know devils from angels."

George feels, not for the first time recently, that he has lived his life encased in shrink-wrap, cushioned from reality.

"Well," he says at last, "at least you tried to find the angels. You went."

"You didn't have much choice."

George looks up at him.

"More than you think," he says.

The trip north after graduation was real, and part of George really did mean to make the grand gesture and leave his country behind. Already, though, sitting in the cheap motel room in northern Vermont, he was missing everything he'd said he was so glad to abandon. It was a wood-paneled room with only one sixty-watt lamp against the darkness. George had taken along a few books among his few possessions, but he couldn't make himself focus on the pages in front of him.

"About 10 o'clock," he says, "I got some change at the front desk and went looking for a pay phone."

Wash James was still awake. George could hear the TV in the background.

He had believed, without admitting it to himself, that his father would come rushing north when Tyler told him (as he knew she would) what his only son was about to do and at least try to talk or bully him out of it.

Wash James, though, obviously was still in his Barco lounger.

He told his son that he was wondering when he was going to call. George said he hadn't planned to call at all, but he wanted to say goodbye.

"Well," Wash told him, "say it."

The silence went on for a long time, and George started worrying about running out of change. He asked Wash if he could reverse the charges.

His father told him he couldn't.

George tried to explain why he was doing it, but his father cut him off.

"You do what you want to do," he said. "It's your life. But I don't give my blessing, if that's what the hell you want, and once you cross that border, I cross you off the list."

George tried to plead with his father, but he ran out of quarters before he could begin to make his case.

He went back to the motel and realized the full extent to which he was alone in the world. By morning, he was well aware of how unprepared he was to trade what seemed like his whole life for a principle.

"It took me two days to get back down there," George says. "The worst part was having to face the old man, knowing that he and I both knew who I was and what my life was going to be.

"I want to think, now, that he played hardball with me because he didn't want to lose me, but I can't be sure. Some of it, with Wash, was he just didn't like to lose at anything, period.

"It's strange, but despite all that talk about writing me off the list, I think he did it anyhow, the day I came back. He'd won, but Wash didn't respect losers. Which would be me."

George pauses and clears his throat.

"We had a pretty good relationship, I think, Wash and me, when all was said and done. And sometimes, I regret the thing I did to get even with him. In the long run, it didn't give me much satisfaction."

The war medals had always been around the house, and Wash didn't say much about them until he became a politician.

By early 1973, with the campaign for lieutenant governor really rolling, George knew what he was going to do. He'd been working for his father's company for more than a year, with time off for four months of active military duty. His life seemed laid out like a flat, straight road, extending beyond the curvature of the Earth.

He found the expression on his father's face, when he would catch Wash unawares for a split second looking at him, to be unbearable.

"I guess I just wanted to win one," George says, "even if the victory was both unheralded and, for the family, pyrrhic."

He sent the tip anonymously to a reporter he knew slightly at the Times-Dispatch. When nothing happened for several days, he sent it to two reporters at the Washington Post who covered Virginia politics.

Finally, a week after the last two letters were sent, a story appeared, on the front of the Post's region section. Then, the local paper picked it up, and it became a brief, all-consuming firestorm that died down only after Wash James' political career had been charred beyond recognition or redemption.

"We all knew he was bullshitting about all the war stuff. I think I figured it out about my junior year," George says.

"I don't think he was even aware he was lying, after a while. I really believe that in some weird inner place, he thought those medals were his."

Outwardly, nothing much changed after a disgraced George Washington James II dropped his bid for lieutenant governor and the Democrats quickly named another man to take his place. Wash was not abandoned by his club or his friends or his family. After a short, self-induced exile with Clara in England and then at their home, he gradually came back to the world with which he'd been perfectly happy in the first place.

"Sometimes, though," George says, "I'd catch him looking at me, and I knew he wondered, but he was afraid to ask. Didn't want to know, I guess."

George is standing and pacing. He shakes his head, as if to clear cobwebs or return from the past.

He turns to Jake and Andrea.

"We need to get the hell out of here."

But then the phone rings. Freeman tells Tim Fairweather not to answer, but he does anyhow, saying it might be his friend, the doctor.

"Tim Fairweather," he says, then listens in silence for several seconds.

After he hangs up the phone, he stands motionless for a few seconds more.

"Maybe you ought to stay inside for just now," he says.

CHAPTER EIGHTEEN

Jake is looking at the clock on the wall across from him. Its face is that of a befuddled George W. Bush, arms akimbo, with "Time to Go" in large letters just beneath the center.

It's just after 2 on what ought to be a quiet Saturday afternoon. On the muted television in the basement that Box has turned on, a college football game is soundlessly, incongruously playing out.

It's been no more than five minutes since Fairweather got the call, and those inside his house did not spend the time wisely, arguing about what they should do next.

The back door leads to a garden, hidden from the street, and Jake supposes Box and Goldstein must have slipped in through the alleyway that bisects the block.

When the door suddenly collapsed inward, Fairweather screamed and ran for the front door, but when Goldstein ordered him to stop, he obeyed. The others stood and sat where they were, more or less stunned. Jake silently cursed his father for not heeding his advice. After the call, Jake had wanted him, his father and Andrea to simply run for it, get in his father's car and head north. But George had hesitated, said, no, they might be out there somewhere, waiting to ambush them, as if they weren't the perfect prey right where they were.

Goldstein found the basement door, opened it and descended, walking backward, his pistol raised. Box, equally well-armed, stood between them and the front door and marched them downstairs.

Goldstein looks much as he did when Jake first saw him, but he seems not to have shaved in a couple of days. He's either wearing the same black suit and white shirt or he has more than one of each. He looks around the room, where everyone's now seated. Both he and Box have pistols with barrels so large Jake feels as if he's staring into a canyon.

'Well, well. One, two, three, four, five, six. Ah, Mr. Hawk. It would have been better, better indeed, if you had left all the others out of it. Do like a sick old dog and go off by yourself to die alone. With our help, of course."

Goldstein laughs, then walks over to Aaron.

"Well, Box," he says, "it looks like you hit something after all."

"Leave him alone," Freeman says. "He doesn't know anything about any of this."

Goldstein moves closer to Aaron, who stares up at him.

"I'm sure you're right," he says, looking down at Freeman's brother, "but I have a feeling his pain will hurt you more than yours would."

He smiles and orders all of them into the middle of the room. Box slides the couch to one side so the pine floor is bare except for a rug. Then, they are ordered to sit there, moving as closely together as possible.

"Please," Tim Fairweather pleads, walking toward Goldstein with his hands up. "Don't . . ."

Goldstein lowers the pistol and shoots Fairweather in the foot. It would be comical, Jake thinks, the way he first hops and then falls to the floor, screaming, if it were some cartoon and not reality. Box is told to gag him, to muffle his screams, and then Fairweather is pushed to the floor, beside the others.

Goldstein looks at the wide-eyed assemblage before him.

"Oh, that?" he says, shrugging his shoulders. "That was just for effect. How are you going to know that I'm a bad, bad man and not some Canadian creampuff come down here to plead for my money back. This guy," and he waves

191

his gun toward Fairweather, who closes his eyes and whimpers, "he just happened to be the nail that popped up, and got hammered."

Jake can feel Andrea shaking, and she seems to be having trouble breathing. He puts his arm around her.

Goldstein turns to him.

"Ah, yes," he says. "My good friend . . . Jake, is it?"

Jake keeps his head down and doesn't respond.

"You were very helpful, Jake," he says. "Not your fault that we weren't able to capture Mr. Hawk, was it? You did your part.

"Although, seeing that you're down here now, I suppose you must have had a change of heart. Perhaps you felt a bit guilty about telling us where he was."

Freeman speaks.

"You don't have to do that."

Goldstein whirls, pointing the gun at him.

"I said, you don't have to do that," Freeman repeats. "I know you made him tell you. I'd have done the same thing. No big deal."

Goldstein laughs.

"Well, it could be a big deal indeed, Mr. Hawk. Could be the biggest, and last, deal in your muddle-headed life."

He turns to Jake again.

"At any rate, no good deed goes unpunished, eh?"

He motions for Freeman to stand.

"Tie his hands," he tells Box, as the others sit on the floor, afraid to move, the silence broken by Fairweather's moans through the gag.

Freeman senses that he is fast approaching the point of no return.

"Wait."

"Yes?" Goldstein moves within a few feet of Freeman, his fingers moving on the gun. Jake can see the sweat on the back of his soiled white shirt.

"I can tell you where my part of it is. If you promise to leave them alone."

"No promises, Mr. Hawk, other than I promise you won't suffer so much. Maybe the first time you beg me to kill you, I'll do it."

Goldstein steps back a few steps, a look of triumph on his face.

"I knew it," he says. "All that bullshit about righteous causes and such. You got your cut, all right. You were playing both ends against the middle, weren't you, Mr. Hawk? Well, sometimes, you can get squashed like that."

Freeman says he won't tell them anything unless the rest are allowed to go unharmed.

"When I have your share in my hands, and a good idea where those sand niggers have gone with the rest," Goldstein says, "then we'll talk about what comes next. I can assure you that, when that blessed moment arrives, you can count on some leniency from the court."

He grins when he says it, and Jake can see the glint of a gold tooth.

Freeman hesitates, then tells him how, after the robbery, he was called by the Palestinian, who told him he would be getting a key in the mail within days, along with directions to a certain security box at a bank in the suburbs. He was told that his help was appreciated, and that he soon would get his reward.

"I didn't want their money," Freeman tells Goldstein. "I didn't know what they were going to do, I swear. I did not know."

"But, the money," Goldstein says, letting it hang.

Freeman says he received an envelope in the mail the next day, with no return address. Inside, was the key, and the directions.

"I went there, and I opened the box, and I saw it," he says.

"And . . . ?"

193

"I left it there. I didn't know what to do. I thought about calling you from somewhere, to tell you where it was, to prove that I didn't have anything to do with any of this."

"Thoughts are very nice, Mr. Hawk, but actions are the only coin of the realm here right now. Actions."

Freeman tells him that he still has the key, in the only bag he brought with him to New Hope, which is in the trunk of his rental car. Goldstein stands behind Andrea and holds his gun half a foot from her head, then sends Box to retrieve the bag.

When he returns, Goldstein takes the key and examines it from all sides, as if appraising its worth.

"I suppose this would count as mitigating circumstances, Mr. Hawk, if you had given it up before there was a gun pointed at your ugly face."

"You were going to kill me, no matter what."

Goldstein nods.

"Probably. Certain actions require certain other actions if the status quo is to be preserved. But there are levels of death and suffering. As you no doubt soon will discover."

He walks back and forth on the worn carpet, as if in thought.

Jake holds Andrea tight; he can feel her shaking. He glances at his father. George has been so still that he forgot momentarily that he was there. He looks suddenly older to Jake, with stubble on his face and his hair barely combed. His body has a slightly sour smell, a combination of age, alcohol and thirty-six hours without a bath. Jake has the fleeting impression that he should be taking care of his father, or at least that someone should.

He doesn't know when the tables turned, but he realizes that somehow they have. George was never the kind of father who took charge, the benevolent despot who acted arbitrarily and decisively in what he judged to be the best interests of his family, never looking back, knowing that he would be right more than he was wrong. Jake had known fathers like that. Growing up, some of his friends had such fathers. They set down rules, with consequences, and they almost never relented. Jake sometimes felt sorry for these friends. Their fathers did not seem to be paragons of virtue, or more than superficially warm and affectionate, and he often thought their tough-minded approach to child-rearing was driven by a desire to make their own lives as simple and seamless as possible.

He once heard his mother and father discussing a man who had sent his oldest son, a few years older than Jake, to Fork Union, a military school up in the hills. He said he wanted to "straighten him out."

"He'll straighten him out all right," Carter said. "When he gets out of there, he'll be less 'straight' than when he left here. He'll go to some college that'll let him in and flunk out in a year after trying to drink enough to make up for lost time. Trust me. I've seen it. It's like these guys think they're back in England, lord of the manor. Send the little buggers off to some prison school in the middle of nowhere and don't see them again until they're all grown and 'straightened out.' "

George tried to take the father's side, but Carter knew what she was talking about, having seen some of it in her own family.

"And yours," she said, giving her husband a meaningful glance.

George's more gentle, democratic mode of child-rearing worked well enough when there were two of them. Carter was the disciplinarian the majority of the time, and George was the soft touch who could be prevailed upon occasionally to intercede.

After Carter's death, though, the balance was lost. There was no one to really quell minor adolescent insurrections. To make matters worse, George was less likely than before to step in, and Jake came to feel that he and his father had both lost the compass that guided their lives.

And, for some reason, George's lack of focus, his inability to control not only his son but also himself, seems to have gotten worse in the past few weeks. Jake has surprised himself and his father by doing better in the void, and he wonders sometimes if he isn't just trying to do well enough to make his father pay attention.

He turns back to George and is struck by something like pity.

"Don't worry, Dad," he says. "It'll be OK. We'll be fine."

He realizes he hasn't called him "Dad" in some time.

George only nods his head.

Jake is shaken from his reverie by Goldstein's voice.

"Son of a bitch," he says. "Son of a bitch."

He turns toward Freeman.

"You're lying to me," he says.

It seems to Jake that Goldstein has been firmly convinced all along that Freeman Hawk has betrayed him. Why, he wonders, forgetting his own precarious position for a moment, would Goldie suddenly be struck by the fact that Freeman had not been completely truthful?

"So that Palestinian, towel-headed fuck just sent you a key, gave you a nice finder's fee for setting me up? I saw the way that guy looked at you. If you'd been on fire, he wouldn't have pissed on you to put it out. Why would he have given you a slice when he didn't have to? You were just another goddamn infidel, Mr. Hawk. Plus, you weren't exactly reachable afterward, were you? God knows, we worked hard enough to find you."

Goldstein moves closer to Freeman, putting the gun just inches from his face. He seems ready to pull the trigger, and Jake closes his eyes.

Freeman says nothing, just looks straight into the barrel of the gun.

196

"Tell me, Mr. Hawk," Goldstein says. "Tell me all. About the money. Once and for all, tell me everything, or it's going to look like an abattoir in here."

"All right. Just don't hurt anyone."

Goldstein says nothing, but he backs away a couple of feet.

Freeman looks up at him.

"It wasn't the Palestinian's money. It was mine."

For years, Freeman Hawk had been stealing.

He saw that it was possible, in his transactions with Goldstein and his associates, to take just a little for himself, and it became like second nature. He hardly thought of it as stealing any more. And it wasn't as if he was using it to buy himself a widescreen TV.

"You saw how I live," he says. "One bedroom, a kitchen, a bathroom, a living room."

Goldstein smiles, the gold tooth flashing briefly.

"Yes. I don't trust anyone, but seeing where you lived, I knew you couldn't be skimming me."

"Well, you were wrong."

Goldstein frowns at this but motions with the pistol for Freeman to continue.

In addition to his work with the Palestinians, he'd been helping out for years, almost since he moved to Montreal, at various soup kitchens, on Thanksgiving and Christmas and whenever else he felt the need to do some sort of non-religious penance. Almost ten years ago, he started helping at Refuge Bleu. It started as a homeless shelter, then grew into three separate shelters, one for men, one for women and another for families. Its volunteers went around the city delivering food and looking for people sleeping in doorways.

As the homeless population grew, fed by immigrants, indigenous people from the north and those fleeing the hopelessness of small towns to the east, Freeman saw that there was almost no way existing resources could keep up.

One day, he came to Marie-Helene, who ran the women's shelter and had slept with him on occasion. He asked her how much was needed to ensure that the disenfranchised have food and shelter and a chance to stand up again. He asked her the morning after they found the old man outside the front door, turned away because they already were ten percent over what the authorities allowed. He seemed to have frozen just in time to avoid death by starvation.

She gave him a figure that exceeded his legitimate annual income and he told her he would see what he could do, that he had come into some family money.

"My family money," Goldstein says.

Freeman tells him that he gave what he could.

"Ten percent, a tithe, just like the good Baptists back home."

But, of course, that barely made a dent.

"How much have I given your tired, your poor, your huddled masses yearning for a fix?" Goldstein asks.

"Little enough," Freeman tells him, looking up, "that you never noticed."

"Well, I thank you, Mr. Hawk, for bringing it to my attention. I am a man who likes to tend to unpaid debts. It is a sign of weakness, I've always believed, to forgive debts. Or anything else."

"They don't even know where it came from. If the sisters knew it came from you, they wouldn't have taken it."

Goldstein considers this briefly.

"Well, I suppose you're right. So, my only way to get something back from this compulsory benevolence is you. I won't get the money back, of course, but there will be an understanding, back in Montreal, about the price for stealing from me."

He frowns again.

"But the key . . ."

Freeman looks up.

"It's real. The box is real. I take a little out, whatever they need, when they need it."

"Ah, yes. I see. And you didn't think it would be . . . right to commingle your actual money with what you stole from me, not to be confused with what you also got from me and the towel-heads for being our, ah, middleman."

Freeman is silent.

"Tell me, Mr. Hawk: How much money is actually in that little box right now?"

"I would guess very little."

"And why is that?"

"Before I left, I gave Refuge Bleu a copy of the key. I told them nothing else was likely to be coming for a while, to use what was there wisely. I don't even know why I kept the original."

Goldstein paces a bit, never taking his eyes off Freeman Hawk.

"Well," he says at last, "I suppose we have come to the end of your tangled web, although God knows I'll never be sure. Maybe, before I'm done with you, before I cut your tongue out, you will tell me even more amazing tales."

He motions to Box.

"Tie him up and gag him. I want him to watch."

Freeman leaps up, but Box smashes him across the face with the pistol. He falls to the floor, conscious and bleeding. He spits something onto the floor, and Jake sees that it is a tooth.

"Careful," Goldstein says, never raising his voice. "I don't want him hurt too badly. I want it all for myself."

On his left, Jake can hear Andrea crying, and he squeezes her more tightly. He hardly notices his father until George is on his feet and charging toward Goldstein. A deafening blast seems to make him fall backward before he's halfway there. As Jake jumps up, he sees Freeman pull the little pistol from his waistband and point it at Goldstein, who looks surprised.

"You, Mr. Hawk?" he says. "A gun . . . ?" And then he's down. Freeman fires three times before Box levels him, firing twice. Jake, running toward the squat man, feels a searing pain in his side and falls, deafened by the noise, between his father and Freeman Hawk.

He can see Box's shoes, inches from his face. He can hear Andrea and Tim Fairweather whimpering in the background. Aaron is moaning. He closes his eyes and waits.

Then, he hears footsteps receding toward the stairs. He is facing in that direction and squints so that he can see through the gap in his eyelids. He's in too much pain to feign death; he can barely breathe.

The last Jake sees of Box is the man's massive body moving up the stairs, almost filling the space. He seems to be shaking his head.

CHAPTER NINETEEN

The morning sun plays off the wallpaper. A light breeze rustles the curtains. In the park below, someone's off his meds.

"Good morning, sleepyhead."

Jake, awakening from another unsettling dream, thinks at first it's his mother.

He opens his eyes and can't suppress a small groan, partly because of the pain, mostly because it's Tyler. He loves his aunt, but her presence means the real world is still there.

She's smiling, but a frown creases her forehead.

"Did you sleep OK?" she asks, and he nods his head. "You should, with all the great drugs they've been giving you. An elephant should sleep well. We need to start cutting back a little, the doctor said."

Jake nods and tries to drift off and find his place again in a story that already is receding as the shouts from below force him to wake up.

"We need to get you up and presentable," Tyler says.

He still needs help getting dressed, and with the bandage, of course. What he feels is slow progress seems to delight his doctor, who never tires of telling him how fortunate he is.

"One inch," he's said three times now, holding his fingers apart in case Jake has forgotten his basic units of measurement. "One inch, and he hits your lung."

Sitting at the dining room table, with the weak sunlight trying to work through the drawn curtains, he chews on a piece of toast smeared with apple jelly. Tyler doesn't nag him to eat like the aunts do. He heard her once, maybe three days ago, tell Melody Carrington as she walked her to the front door, "When he's hungry, he'll eat."

Today, he rediscovers the joy of scrambled eggs. He realizes that, even if he tries to will himself to shut down, his traitorous body won't let him. He is hungry.

He looks up, across the table, where Tyler smiles and says nothing.

The local paper's reporters have been relatively considerate and seem to have accepted Tyler's demand that they stop trying to contact Jake until he has "gotten his strength back and feels like talking." They both wish the national and international news media would be as accommodating and are thankful for the ability to screen calls. When Jake looks out at the park now, he always sees several people with cameras of various sizes, some of them seemingly focused on his bedroom window twenty-four hours a day. One grainy picture of himself, looking down, has been shown repeatedly on what Tyler calls the catfish news shows, the bottom-feeders.

God knows he's had to talk enough, first at the hospital in New Hope, then at St. Mary's in Richmond and once so far here. He sometimes isn't sure if he's talking to local police, Canadian authorities, the FBI or representatives of some unknown federal entity.

They seem to accept his story that he and Andrea knew nothing about Freeman Hawk's illegal activities in Canada, and that he and George were letting Freeman stay with them only because he was an old college friend of his father's. He even tells them about the visit from Box and Goldie, but he leaves out the part where Goldie details Freeman's longtime career as a drug middleman.

The Canadians are more interested in the organized crime aspect, the local cops want to know about the shootout, and the FBI and the other guys are focusing on terrorism. They ask him, over and over, for more details about the Palestinian. Jake hopes he's finally convinced them that they've emptied his memory bank concerning the Palestinian, and that they are at least mostly sure that neither he nor George were part of some cabal aiding people one or two degrees of separation from the demise of the World Trade Center.

The Richmond investigators seem only marginally interested in the fact that he himself has a criminal record.

"I doubt that they're intending to send you to Guantanamo," Tyler said at one point, then quickly added, "bad joke."

Even though she hasn't lived in the U.S. for more than two decades, she is more upset than Jake about Bush's reelection.

"How can these morons do that? A chimp would've been a better choice," she demanded of one FBI agent, who stayed scrupulously neutral and poker-faced on the subject.

After that round of questioning ended, Jake told her, "Keep it up, Tyler, and they'll be sending you to Guantanamo."

She looked at him in surprise, obviously pleased that her nephew had exhibited the first sign of a sense of humor since the shooting. She has waited in vain for another.

Jake had awakened in a North Carolina hospital, with tubes running from him in all directions. They kept him medicated so heavily that he didn't know what was going on for a couple of days. Gradually, most of the nightmare came back to him, and Tyler and the occasional law enforcement figure filled him in on the aftermath.

Freeman Hawk was gone before the first ambulance got there. In death, he seems to fill all the American and Canadian news media's requirements for Big Story. Everyone from the *New York Times* on down has seized on it. "A ghost from the Vietnam era emerges forty years later, linking a tragic war with the nightmare of 9/11," intoned one somber network news anchor.

They don't know all the details about what Freeman Hawk did and who he helped. Jake isn't sure anyone is ever really going to know, but there is enough, Tyler says, to keep fat, greasy fucks with hundred-pound cameras hanging out in the park for some time to come.

Aaron Hawk is still being questioned by the same people who are grilling Jake, who hopes Aaron has someone as good as Tyler around to serve as some kind of buffer. He doubts it, though. He already has seen Aaron on two of the catfish shows, looking uncomfortable in a suit, handling questions about his late brother with a North Carolina mill-town accent that sounds even slower on TV than it did in person. He seems, from what Jake hears and reads, to be looking for someone, somewhere to sue, and he smiles at inappropriate moments, as if wishing to satisfy his unseen audience. Tyler says she's pretty sure the "news" programs he's on pay their guests.

"I didn't know nothin' about those turrists," he says more than once.

If the authorities weren't sure Aaron Hawk had anything to do with his brother's lawless life, they had fewer doubts about Tim Fairweather.

Fairweather was seen often on the news shows. The clip they usually showed was of him being led into the court-room for his arraignment, limping badly, wearing a bright orange jumpsuit, his thinning hair matted to his forehead. There also were photos of him from family albums and yearbooks, all the way back to college days. In one par-ticularly overused shot, circa 1970, he and George stand on either side of Freeman Hawk, their arms linked around each other's shoulders. Fairweather is wearing a T-shirt with "Nixon Sucks" and an image of the president imprinted on it.

Someone was able to videotape Fairweather's living room and sell the tape to one of the cable news networks. The camera lingers over various signs and posters advocating the speedy demise of George W. Bush.

New Hope College placed Fairweather on unpaid leave almost immediately, and the president issued a statement declaring that New Hope definitely did not in any way support anyone who facilitated "the tragic events of September 11" and most assuredly did not advocate the overthrow of the government.

There was enough in Fairweather's house, though, to convince the FBI that he was a threat, and he seems to have disappeared.

"Free trip to Cuba," Tyler said, shaking her head as she and Jake watched the evening news.

Tyler came to Richmond by herself. Maria's back in Oaxaca, and Tyler calls her every day. It was best, they decided, that she come alone, as no one knows how long she'll be needed.

The death of Robert Goldstein was more noted in Canada than in the U.S., where he had been a "person of interest" for years in Montreal's underworld. He barely had a criminal record at all.

But that was before the fiction of his background unraveled, which it quickly did after his death, abetted by a high school yearbook and a few family photos that Goldstein had for some reason kept with him since 1967.

Robert Goldstein, it was discovered soon after his death, was not Robert Goldstein at all. His first name, it turned out, was about the only thing that wasn't invented.

He wasn't from a wealthy New York family. He wasn't Jewish. He had been born in a small upstate town along the Hudson River as Robert Herr. His mother was a waitress and his father was unknown. He had been in and out of trouble since junior high school and dropped out before he finished the eleventh grade, the year his mother died of a drug overdose.

An older half-sister was the closest relative anyone could find.

"He was smart," the half-sister said as the smoke from her cigarette wafted between her face and the camera. "He didn't like school much, because he didn't put up with a lot of shit—pardon my French. But he was always reading, that one. He was what you call self-educated. The reading, you know, it made him seem kind of, like, geeky, and him being such a skinny little fu . . . fella, he got beat up a lot. Not a lot of readers around here. I think being picked on might have been what led him to crime. Not that there's a lot of other options in this place, you know?"

At that point, the camera panned to the town behind them, most of whose old brick buildings seemed to have long since been abandoned.

The strange thing, the half-sister said, was that the thing she remembered him reading about most, the thing that seemed almost like an obsession, was Nazi Germany.

"He was always reading about Adolf Hitler and all that World War II stuff, the Holocaust and all," she said. "I think he had a swastika in his room when he was in junior high. Yeah, I'm sure of it."

She smiled for the first time in the interview, and the missing front tooth became visible.

"I didn't expect Bobby to show up as no Jew," she said, "although he did have kind of curly hair. Who knows? He might of been one."

Her laugh quickly turns into a wrenching cough, and the interview ends.

No one seemed to know what happened to Bobby Herr in the three years between his mostly unremarked departure from the dying river town and his reappearance in Montreal as Robert Goldstein. And no one in Montreal remembered him as anything except the skinny Jewish kid who claimed to be there because of Vietnam.

"Everybody back then," a veteran police officer from Montreal said, "did not come to Canada for the purest of reasons."

Box just disappeared. It seemed improbable, considering his size and general appearance, that he would go unnoticed. Maybe, somebody conjectured, he went to the Philippines. He had some family there. Or maybe he was still somewhere in the United States, afraid to cross, afraid to go back to a place where he was recognizable to so many.

Jake hasn't seen or spoken with Andrea in the past three weeks. He has tried to call her three times. The last time, her mother told him she was going to get an injunction, and that if he called again, he would be arrested.

The last thing he remembers of her is the feel of her body next to his that day, rocking back and forth in a steady, almost imperceptible rhythm. She seemed to be humming something, but he never could figure out what it was. When he would tell her, again, that everything was going to be all right, she would nod her head slightly, then continue rocking and humming.

Four days ago, he got an unexpected visit. When Tyler took the call and told him someone named Peter Fallon was in the lobby and wanted to come up and see him, Jake shook his head; but curiosity got the better of him, and he told Tyler it was OK.

Fallon, when he came into Pete's room with Tyler standing behind him (Jake had given her a brief rundown of their past as Fallon took the elevator to the sixth floor), appeared more serious than Jake ever remembered seeing him.

"How you doin'?" he asked, almost shyly.

Jake said he was just glad to be alive.

"Yeah. Me, too," Fallon said, and Jake didn't want to ask which one of them he was glad for.

They were silent for a time.

"Call me if you need anything," Tyler said on the way out.

Fallon moved closer to the chair where Jake was sitting in a robe and slippers. He hated looking like an invalid, but changing clothes had become a daily agony he put off as long as he could.

"The thing is," Fallon said, "Andrea asked me to come."

Jake sat up a little.

"It's OK. I mean, we're past history, you know, me and her. Nothing to be upset about now. Just friends."

He fixed his gaze on the window.

"Look, I was pissed, OK? But it was more like I resented being moved on."

Jake regarded his former tormentor, not sure where the conversation was going.

Fallon nodded his head, as if agreeing with some inner voice.

"Yeah," he said, "I can be a jerk. No denying that."

"But, about Andrea . . ." Jake reminded him.

"Oh, yeah. Well, seeing as how I never did get on her mom's shit list, unlike you, they let me come by last week."

Andrea had been "pretty drugged up," he said, and he hadn't been allowed to talk to her for long.

Before her mother made him leave, Andrea told Pete Fallon that he had to get in touch with Jake.

"It's like she was a prisoner there," he said. "She didn't have a cell phone or nothing. She said they put her in Tucker's after she went nuts down there, but they didn't keep her but for a week or so. But she said her folks were going to send her away, to some kind of school or something."

Jake knew about the "school" where Andrea's parents had almost sent her after her breakdown at Madison Hall.

"Anyhow, she wanted me to tell you she's all right, that they're taking good care of her, that you shouldn't worry about her."

Jake thought to himself, "Her? What about me?" But he kept silent. He knew enough, from what he'd seen on television and heard second- and third-hand, that Andrea must have been more or less out of it by the time the police came. She was stopped half a block away, hiding behind a holly bush, in her underwear. Her jeans and blouse, splattered with blood, had been shed along the way.

"Thing is," Pete Fallon told him, "she's not right. I mean, she needs some help."

Jake couldn't deny that, but he wondered if she was going to get any kind of meaningful help, and he still felt that he could make her right, just by holding her. It wouldn't do him any harm, either.

"By the way," Fallon said, not seeming to know how to broach the subject, "that day on the island, the gunfire. Was that . . . ?"

Jake laughs, then winces.

"Me? No."

"Then who?"

"I don't know," Jake said. He thought he might know who, but he just didn't know why, and everyone was dead, anyhow.

Fallon quickly ran out of things to say.

As he got up to leave, he awkwardly stuck out his hand.

Jake took it, looking up.

"Get well, OK?" he said.

Jake nodded, and looked down again. Then, Fallon was down the hall, opening the front door to leave.

"Thanks," he called out, but Fallon was already gone. He assumed that Andrea Cross had something to do with Pete Fallon's sudden and inexplicable desire to make peace. It felt like some final, irreciprocal gift.

Today, the sun feels good as it works its way into afternoon, not clearing the horizon by much, flooding Jake's room. The bells from the cathedral are background music as Jake drifts in and out of sleep in his chair overlooking the park.

He doesn't hear Tyler until she's standing right behind him.

"Jake," she says, putting her hands on his shoulders. "Buddy, do you want to go? You know, we talked about going today, but if you don't feel up to it, I understand?"

"No," he says, shaking his head as he wakes from a dream about Andrea, "I'm ready. Let's go."

She finds him a coat, and he realizes as he works his arms into it slowly and painfully that he hasn't been outside in a week, since the last doctor's visit. The radiators in the Warwick put out so much heat that his window is open slightly, and he can smell autumn outside, leaves and wood smoke. As much as he doesn't want to make this trip, he's ready to get outside the apartment for a while.

He's steady enough to walk to the elevator. When they get off in the lobby, two of the Aunts are there, along with another longtime resident, a man in his seventies who ministers to a small Episcopal church. He and his wife have just returned from services.

Before Tyler leads Jake to the more private back entrance and goes to get the car, they all make much of him, telling him how well he looks, how much they've missed him.

Melody Carrington says she'll come by later with some cookies. She moves close and motions for him to lean down.

"You're going to be OK," she says, almost in a whisper. "You're going to have a good life."

She squeezes his hand and steps back.

"I hope so," he says.

He insists on getting into the car himself, even if the dip down does cause him more pain than he can hide. When Tyler reaches across to help him with the seatbelt, he thinks to himself that this must be what getting old is like. He did the same thing once when he and George took Mrs. Hamilton from the Warwick to her favorite restaurant to celebrate her ninetieth birthday.

"OK," Tyler says, looking straight ahead. "Here we go."

The trip only takes five minutes. They could have walked it in less than fifteen, if Jake had been well.

He rejects her offer to help him lift himself out of the car, and then the two of them walk along, side by side. The path is really a road, wide enough for traffic. The maples are barely past their peak, something Tyler remarks on. Jake is wishing they weren't so damn beautiful, that the sun wasn't shining, or that this wasn't the most perfect fall day imaginable.

They have to walk almost a quarter-mile, which is farther than Jake has managed since he was shot. He is pleased that he is able to do it, although his legs are rubbery by the time they get there.

"Turn right here," Tyler says softly.

They climb a couple of steps, and then the plot is directly in front of them.

On the left, the headstone says "Malachi James" with "Sarah Smoot James" beside it.

Among the others Jameses, mostly Malachi and Sarah's children, are the stones for George Washington James and "beloved wife" Virginia Booker James. Farther back are the ones for "George Washington 'Wash' James II" and "Clara Worthington James."

The last one still has fresh earth around it, and there are still some flowers. Someone has put fresh mums there, all orange and purple.

Jake steps forward and runs his hands along the cool letters grooved into granite, tracing his father's name.

Carved in stone, he thinks. No going back.

Tyler stands behind him and puts her arms around him. She leans her head forward, pressing it into his backbone.

He had no chance to attend the funeral. Even with a four-day gap, he was still hooked to tubes in intensive care at

MCV. Gunshot wounds, the doctor told Tyler, who was there along with Carter's brother, are serious business.

"So is his father's funeral," Tyler said, but she knew the doctor was right.

Jake doesn't remember much about the way things ended at Tim Fairweather's. He has racked his brain, trying to recall everything about the last time he saw George James, and it isn't much. His father's inexplicable charge toward Goldie, the way he lurched back like a fish suddenly and violently hooked. And then Jake was rushing forward, going toward his father, and then the pain, the burning, the smell and the moaning—perhaps one of those voices belonging to his father. The last thing he saw before he passed out was Box's shiny shoes and then the man himself in retreat.

He was in the hospital at MCV for five days before they told him about it, but he knew already. Even sedated, he couldn't miss all the whispered conversations outside his open door, the way people treated him as if he were fine porcelain. He heard the word "funeral" more than once. He knew, but he felt that if no one actually said it, maybe it didn't happen. Maybe it was a dream. Don't ask, don't tell.

On the fifth day, Tyler came in and shut the door too quietly behind her.

"There's no easy way . . ." she started, and he wanted to put his hands over his ears, but he just nodded. It was weird. He had cried about a number of things, many of them trivial, in the last few years, but he stayed dry as a bone when Tyler told him.

Only now, with the evidence a foot from his face as he kneels on the stone, does he yield.

CHAPTER TWENTY

The sky is so blue and seems so close that he feels almost oppressed by it, as if it might lower itself a bit more and smother him.

The weather has finally broken, for the time being. Tyler has told him about the abrupt change from wet to dry, how everyone comes out and celebrates the sun.

The colors were what got him at first. There were times, on cloudy days, when the colors made him think that the sun was out. His life in Richmond seems now like old TV movies with washed-out hues, and this was high definition.

He speaks to two of the vendors who wait patiently along the edge of the zócalo with their ceramics and cotton fabric, hoping the tourists will be here today. He has become familiar with many of the small, dark, weather-beaten men he sees here every day. His Spanish has improved, or at least has adjusted to the local dialect. Tyler has told him he has a natural gift, that he already speaks it better than she does after all these years. When she says that, Maria giggles and agrees.

"You should be in school," one of the vendors says, jokingly admonishing him for his truancy.

"Soon," Jake says. "Soon."

Leaving Richmond wasn't something he planned.

A week after he visited George's grave, he and Tyler went to Anderson Stokes' office. The lawyer had a window office in one of the newer buildings separated from the James

River by the canal and the railroad tracks. Jake, looking out, could see an egret far below, sitting on a rock and waiting for dinner to swim past.

Stokes told them how sorry he was about everything. He said everyone was so proud of George for doing "what he did," and that the club was talking about starting a fund for a scholarship in his name.

Jake doesn't necessarily think of his father as heroic. He will never know what went through George James' head just before he made his charge, and he doesn't know whether the distraction of his father being shot is what enabled Freeman Hawk to shoot and kill Goldstein.

He doesn't really care.

But at the lawyer's office, he nodded and grunted an almost unintelligible "thank you."

Then, Anderson Stokes' expression, which already had gone from companionable to sorrowful, changed again, to business mode.

"I don't know how much your dad—your brother—told you about Old Dominion Hams."

"We know he was selling it," Tyler speaks up. "I signed papers. We assume Jake and I are the only inheritors of his estate."

"Yes, his estate." Stokes seemed to grimace as if the word caused him pain.

Jake looked at the man, who had been in his parents' home many times, had shared drinks with George at the Warwick, and he saw how he avoided eye contact.

"What?" he asked.

The Old Dominion Ham Company, it turned out, had been losing money for some time, slowly for several years but, in what Stokes called "the stressed economic conditions of the early twenty-first century," much more quickly.

"He sold it to pay off debts. I don't think even he knew the true measure of his debt until the time of the sale. George never was much for paying attention to the bottom line. No offense."

"So," Tyler asked, and Jake could see that her hands were gripping the arms of the mahogany chair, "what's left, after everything's paid off?"

Stokes can't seem to get to the bottom line himself, taking side excursions to explain how the company tried to expand its export business too quickly, got overextended, couldn't reverse itself.

"And, of course, economies of scale," Stokes said, as if everyone knew what a problem those could be.

"I suppose he was going to tell you, but it was painful for him."

Tyler, still gripping the chair's arms as if she's afraid she might hurtle forward and strangle Stokes if she lets go, interrupts him.

"Do you think," she says, her voice a low growl, "you could possibly get to the fucking point?"

The point at which Anderson Stokes finally arrived was the one at which there were virtually no assets left after the Old Dominion Ham Company had paid all its debts.

"I mean, there might be more debtors out there, for all we know," he says, "but you can't squeeze blood from a stone."

He said he supposed the apartment was safe "for the time being," and that Jake should check with Social Security to see what he might be entitled to as a sixteen-year-old without parents.

"Good God," was all Tyler said. Jake said nothing.

There was more conversation, mostly from the lawyer, who seemed capable of spending an almost unlimited amount of time answering even the simplest question.

Jake hadn't given the money much thought, but now he knew he'd always assumed that he would be taken care of, that no matter how awful present circumstances were, there always would be the Old Dominion Ham Company, and then the money his father got for selling it.

It was funny, in a way, when he had time to digest it. His father had seen the company as something of an albatross, and he himself had never even considered that he might someday run it himself. Now, a world in which he would have been the future heir to a thriving business, the end product of four generations of Jameses' sweat and business acumen, didn't seem so bad after all.

"How does that happen?" Tyler said as they left the lawyer's office. "How do you turn something into nothing?"

Jake wondered, still wonders, when his father was going to tell him.

Tyler broke the news to Carrie Bass, whose mourning was of a much shorter duration than Jake's, but even she was taken aback.

"He never told me," she assured him. "I woke up once, not long before . . . before it happened, and he wasn't there. I saw the light and went into the den, and he'd obviously been crying. He said it was nothing, just a lot of stress, selling the business and all."

Carrie told Jake that she hoped they'd still be friends, that she'd check on him from time to time.

"What are you going to do?" she asked.

When he said he didn't really know, she'd only offered, "Neither do I, kid. Neither do I."

His uncle, St. John Bessette, said he was "there for you," but he and George had never been close, and Jake had only been in the man's house on maybe a dozen occasions. Jake thought he might have stepped up, if Jake had asked, but he didn't.

The Aunts were more willing than anyone else in Richmond to take him to their collective bosom. Melody Carrington flatly told him he could move in with her, for free, until he graduated from high school, no questions asked.

"Honey," she said, "if you can stand it, I'd love to have you."

He might have done it. Tyler explained to him how much just the condo fees and taxes were, and he knew the place in which he and his father had lived was going up for sale.

But they weren't even out of the building where the will was read when Tyler told him, "Sweetie, you're coming home with me."

He didn't agree to it at first, and maybe he wouldn't have if Andrea Cross were still in town, or the money he'd expected hadn't disappeared.

It wasn't easy. He was still on probation, and Tyler's domestic situation probably would not have pleased the Richmond judge who made the final decision.

"Well," he said after Tyler had made her case, "you are his aunt. And I don't see anybody else in the family volunteering."

He told Jake that he had been very fond of his father, and that he hated to see the last of the Jameses leave Richmond. Jake had never thought of himself before as the last of anything, and he wanted to tell the judge he wouldn't be the last, but he let it slide.

Packing was difficult. He didn't even know what kind of climate to expect, having been there only once, but Tyler helped him with that.

He went by and said goodbye to Melody Carrington, who teared up and caused Jake to do the same.

He tried one last time to reached Andrea through her mother, who hung up on him.

There was a little money in a cap account and George's checking account, and he and Tyler conspired to mail that ahead to Maria for possible future use.

But when Jacob Malachi James boarded the flight to Houston in mid-December, he left most of his first sixteen years behind.

"If you travel light," Tyler told him as they were making final decisions about what to take, "you can travel fast. You're going to need to travel fast. We all are. I don't think this is the American century, kid, or at least not the United States century."

He arrived in Oaxaca in time for Christmas, for Noche de Rabanes and all the rest of the elaborate pageantry, much more centered on religion than any Christmas he had experienced before.

"People here really believe," Tyler said.

He's GOING to finish his school year through a correspondence course. Then, Tyler said, they'll figure out how "and in what language" he'll complete high school "which you definitely are going to do."

He's been amazed at the life she leads. She and Maria get along better than any couple Jake's known, including his own parents, and their friends seem capable of talking all night long about art or politics or even religion, though they are much less believing than the people who line the streets on parade days and fill the golden churches on Sundays. Most of it is over his head, whether it's in Spanish or English.

"You're famous," he said to her one day, after the three of them have watched an interview with Tyler on a television station run by the university.

"Nah," she said, and she almost seemed to blush. "I'm not famous. I'm only well-known, and just around here. It's a big world, buddy. Nobody gets to be famous everywhere. And sometimes it's better just to be happy."

Jake can see the sense in that, and he understands what she was saying when she told him, when he was trying to decide whether to come to Mexico, that the distraction might be good for him.

He can go for hours on end without thinking about his father and mother, or Andrea. As he confronts his father's death, inching into it as if it were a chilling stream, getting accustomed to it, he realizes that Andrea might be lost forever, but that he can survive that loss.

It hits him at odd times. He'll see a middle-aged tourist with the same general appearance or the same walk, or he'll see some smartly dressed woman shopping for jewelry. Sometimes it's just a hand gesture or part of a sentence that reminds him of George or Carter. Last night, for the first time since his arrival, he slept all the way through instead of waking in the small hours, when everything comes back to him with more weight than it ever has in daylight.

He doesn't really have a plan or more than a thimble of hope. He doesn't wake up in the morning feeling noticeably better than he did the day before, but he's pretty sure he's better than he was a month ago, and that he's improving somehow, week by week.

He appreciates that Tyler never treats him as if he's going to break. No one does. All around him are people who seem to be working harder than anyone he knew back home just to have food and shelter. And some of them, he sees, don't always have food and shelter.

"If you plan to do harm to yourself," she told him one day, offhandedly, as they were at the market, buying vegetables and fruit for dinner, "be sure you do it because you just can't take it anymore. Don't do it to get attention, or because you feel sorry for yourself. Look around. This is the world."

Then she turned to him and grinned.

"And for God's sake, don't do it in the apartment. I hate mess."

He didn't smile, but he didn't resent it. Rather, he was grateful that she didn't feel the need to tiptoe. He was grateful that she understood that he was mending.

One day, after she told him about how she wound up in Oaxaca, she said that for some time she'd considered herself an exile.

"Oh, I could go back," she said. "It'd probably be easy now. But they'd make sure it was on their terms. I wouldn't be the artist. I'd be the lesbian artist. We'd have to be careful where we showed affection, have to be in the right group. We'd be fodder for cocktail party chit-chat. Here, I can just be the artist. Maybe they always make allowances for foreigners. We're supposed to be different. Whatever, I appreciate it. This is home. No returns."

Jake thinks of himself as an exile, too. He knows that his uncle or some friend's parents probably would give him a place to stay, but more and more he doubts he'll ever feel comfortable in Richmond again.

"The best people in the world," Tyler is fond of telling him, "are exiles of one kind or another."

He isn't sure if that's true, but he's willing to work with it for now.

He returns to the villa. Maria has gone to work, and Tyler's in her studio. When he stops to say good morning, she tells him that Guillermo came by and was asking for him.

"I told him to come by later, that you'd be back by mid-morning."

Not fifteen minutes later, there's a knock on the door.

The little boy is nine. With his skinny body and matchstick arms and legs, he looks younger, but in Jake's eyes, he seems almost grown.

Jake greets him in Spanish, and the boy's smile is as natural and undiminished as the sun itself.

Guillermo's mother does some housework for Tyler and Maria. They're from Guatemala. She started bringing her son with her to help with the work, and one day Jake asked him how old he was, then what sports he liked.

The boy loved baseball, it turned out, and the two of them would talk in Spanish about the game. Guillermo also was a natural runner, and twice so far Jake has gone with him on a five-mile course the boy has mapped out for himself.

Guillermo, he discovers quickly, is very bright. He only goes to school sporadically, when he can, but Jake knows enough Spanish to see that he can read and write at a level beyond his years.

Jake asked him one day if he'd like to learn English.

The boy nodded his head enthusiastically, and so they began.

Every morning, Guillermo comes by, and Jake teaches him more and more. Tyler is able to find a couple of English grammar books. Guillermo, in exchange, is teaching Jake to play chess. Jake has no idea where he learned it. When he asks, the boy shrugs and says here and there. Jake has not been able to beat him yet.

Guillermo and his mother are alone. They lived in an Indian village in the hills where not even Spanish was spoken. His father died three years ago in the desert over the border in El Norte, part of a group led across the river by a coyote and then abandoned without enough water. Two younger brothers died before they were two.

Guillermo, Jake learns, is not even his birth name, just the one he's adopted here in Oaxaca, to seem less foreign. His mother has told Tyler, in the broken Spanish she has had to learn in the past three years, that Guillermo is the man of the family.

The younger boy does not smile in an obsequious manner or seem embarrassed when this is mentioned. He only shrugs, in acceptance rather than resignation, his small shoulders squared up, and says "si."

He is absorbing English as quickly as Jake can immerse him in it. Today, for the second time, he asks Guillermo questions in English.

"What do you want to do when you are a man?"

Guillermo doesn't hesitate.

"Go to United States America."

"The United States *of* America. What will you do when you get there?" Jake has to repeat the second part, but then the boy understands.

"Work," he says. "I work. I work . . . hard."

"Maybe you can take my place," Jake says, but he sees that the boy doesn't get the joke.

The lesson lasts an hour and a half. Then, Guillermo accepts the invitation to have lunch with Tyler, Maria and Jake. He always demurs, out of politeness; they always insist. He eats the way he always does, afraid to show how hungry he is but unable to do so. Tyler always makes enough so that he can, after some weak protests, take some back.

Jake walks with him a couple of blocks. They're silent until the boy turns to him and asks, in his newfound English, "What . . . what you will do?"

"It's 'What will you do?' " Then Jake realizes he's asking a serious question, one Jake has been asking himself.

Tyler has told him that the mere fact that he speaks fluent Spanish will take him far. He has been constantly amused by the way grateful American tourists tip him when he offers to translate, to facilitate, when they try to haggle with the vendors. Because he is Anglo, they trust him when he says a price is fair. Sometimes, the vendors also give him a small tip, because he tends to nudge the final settlement in their favor when he can. One man wanted him to run his stand for him, selling jewelry and cotton goods. He is considering the offer, although he means to heed Tyler's admonition that school comes first.

"What will I do?" he repeats the question as he and Guillermo stop in the street and the boy looks up at him with wide eyes.

"I work," Jake says, with a small smile. "I work hard."

OTHER TITLES BY HOWARD OWEN

"Quietly enchanting . . . *Littlejohn* remains a warm and generous novel, a heartfelt celebration of the human spirit."

—*The New York Times*

"A wise, warm, deeply satisfying story that resonates with imagery invoking the spiritual tradition of such Southern writers as Faulkner and Flannery O'Connor."

—*Publishers Weekly*

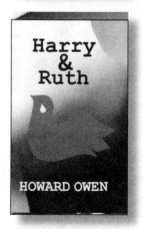

"Owen's strong fifth novel depicts two elderly lovers tying up loose ends and saying good-bye. An interwoven narrative, meanwhile, depicts their life-long connection. A complicated drama, told with compassion and humor."

—*Kirkus*

"In his sixth novel, Owen draws twenty years of experience as a newspaper sports editor to fashion a touching story of fathers, sons, and baseball that emphasizes the irrevocable ties of blood. The pace is leisurely, the revelations apt and unexpected and the coverage of professional baseball rings absolutely true."

—*Publishers Weekly*

"Spurred by a nighttime encounter with a mysterious old man, a faded football hero-cum-long-distance trucker risks everything to become a fiction writer. Owen's portrayal of the agonies an aspiring writer faces are definitely nerve-wracking."

—*Publishers Weekly*

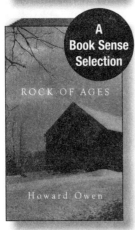

"The prodigal daughter of Owen's Littlejohn, returns to her birthplace hoping to sell Littlejohn's house. Her homecoming is complicated by the drowning of her elderly cousin. A haunting murder mystery."

—*Publishers Weekly*